Contents

Transcendents Vol. 1

The Drug

Where should I start? The prison system? The prisoners? The drug trials? Or the actual drug itself, Copoxydrate? Life as we know it has changed. Society has changed. But everyone is oblivious. Who has changed it? The few? Pfff! Now the few privileged aren't the few anymore. They've created a new small number of people, if we can still call them that. I can't tell you how life is going to look next, but I can tell you what I saw.

*****

My first day on the wing was extremely exciting. You have no idea what to expect on the inside of a prison. The documentaries and prison programmes show people preying on the ones weaker than themselves and others who live to get off their face and fight. I know there are other sides to these individuals as I have sometimes strayed on to the national 'prison' paper the *Inside Watch* online and seen some fantastic works of art submitted to the *'Whistler Awards'*. Reading the Inside Watch fascinated me as their views were so varied, sometimes polarising. I wondered how they could put together such great works of art and write with such conviction in such a hopeless, degrading place of residence. When a friend, who was unemployed, said that they saw a job vacancy at this prison I quickly made my exit to create a CV and submit it. I worked for my dad so I knew if it fell through, or I couldn't handle it I could step back into my old role after several "I told you so's". As I tapped away on my laptop

my heart was in my mouth as I was worried yet thrilled at the possibility I could be walking around a prison. I hoped for a positive response and after 2 days I got the interview, did the training and now I was shadowing an 'experienced' officer. I could see that the officer, O'Brian, that I was shadowing was not liked by the prisoners. He was barking orders to them as we passed. "Don't do that!" "Clear off from here!". I could tell from the looks on their faces and the disdain in his voice that this wasn't a show for me, this was real. I hoped that I wouldn't be on this wing as he was explicit that this was 'his wing'.
That statement didn't end at the prisoners, oh no, it extended to the other officers that were on the wing. As they all gathered round him, laughing at his jokes and recalling his stories *for* him. These stories seemed to consist of "remember when you smashed that inmates head off his bunk when he refused an order?"
Another officer chimed in "he had to be airlifted to the hospital". The first officer went on to say "he was begging to be transferred out of the prison when he regained consciousness and came back to his senses". A wretched throaty laugh, that seemed full of fake machismo, escaped from the first officer. I mustered up my best ad hoc sadistic laugh just to fit in. Another one was "hey, there's that plastic gangster you made squeal from the chicken hook" (this is an outlawed move where the arm of the offender is wrenched up his back with just the control of his thumb and the back of his hand which gives you the chicken wing look. It is excruciating to say the least and can easily tear the rotator cuff in the

shoulder and even dislocate or break it. Sometimes 2 officers do both arms). "He hasn't so much as said boo since. His shoulder and wrist must still be in a bad way as he hasn't been to the gym or done his circuits on the yard." O'Brian just said, "shunt be a mouthy cunt then." Case closed.

*****

Shadowing over, I had earned my own set of keys. Yayy! Unfortunately, I have been stationed on A wing with O'Brian. We are briefed daily with relevant and, sometimes irrelevant, detail and information regarding prisoners and protocol. Who's got what roles and responsibilities today and then released to the house blocks. I didn't want to be ostracised by O'Brian and gang so out of earshot of the prisoners I would stroke O'Brian's ego and speak highly of him to the others as I could tell they would be quick to tell O'Brian if I said anything to the contrary. I also believed he kept his rein through physically manhandling other officers. He is of a stocky build, I'm 6 foot even and he is slightly shorter than me but appears taller through demeaner. He must be in his 50's with the old rugby players build with a strong pot belly and a huge set of hands that could encase my face like the things with the tail in the alien films that inserts an egg in your stomach. His balding shaved grey head and extremely broad square jaw makes you think twice about trying to throw a punch at it.

I generally kept on the move and looked for any 'in' with the prisoners as this is what I was here for. I began to try and categorise the prisoners. I love to people watch anyway and always found it fun. I started the categories to keep myself safe as I didn't want to be one of the photos that they show you during training. Images of officers who have been slashed up, stabbed here, there and everywhere, copious amounts of blood and battered and bruised faces. Not for me, no sir-ree.

The largest group seemed to be those I came to be told were suspected of using drugs, both illicit and prescribed (mainly not prescribed to them). The most notable group were the lads that were self-proclaimed 'gym heads' and I was told by colleagues that these tend to be the movers and shakers. Intelligence suggests that these lads organise and deal drugs, have access to mobile phones and put 'hits' out on each other, those that are in debt to them and cannot pay and, unbelievably, officers. Hits, I found out through working on the wing, witnessing incidents on top of talks with staff and prisoners, range from throwing urine, smearing faeces in faces of opponents to slashings with makeshift knives and physical assaults. There were subgroups within these categories, but I generally just worked off attitude at that time. I had some cracking jokes with the prisoners, and I had spilled my guts laughing, on the flip side I heard some sad and horrific stories and also had some in-depth talks, those are the ones I liked the most. I could see O'Brian and Co. didn't like my

engagement with the prisoners and I was getting fearful.
One morning I was sat in my car in the car park before my shift started and I decided that I was going to knock the job on the head. I thought I would just go back to my dad's gardening business. Really and truly, I had accomplished what I wanted. See what prison life is like, talk to the lads and keep yourself safe. Done, done, done. I knew this wasn't a job for life. I went and sat in the morning meeting as usual and was shocked at what I heard. Scandal? What does she mean? I was preoccupied with my decision that I didn't hear the beginning but the number one governor took over from the security governor and was livid, seething. She just couldn't control it. She spoke of something regarding staff using some sort of drug to get control of inmates. It wasn't the use of the drug but the alleged abuse of it. Apparently, inmates had been left after being administered with high doses. There were allegations that some of the prisoners were being constantly administered so they were left in a stupor in their cell, all alone and at times, missing meals due to being out of it. I didn't catch the name of the drug but the details made me slightly recall something I had heard, here and there, on the news around 18 months ago. The governor went on to mention the treatment of some of the prisoners and I had been aware of the ones on my wing but the other officers said they were off their head on drugs and I, due to living a rather sheltered life, just took their more experienced word for it and banked it for the future as drug behaviour. They were a strange bunch the ones I had laid my eyes on. They were one of the

subgroups I spoke of, or didn't speak of, earlier. She went on and on and started to show us slides of their photos on a wall screen. Some had videos that followed their before and after prison photos. Videos that showed different behaviour whether it was from body cam footage, wing CCTV, media coverage of trials, stuff that had been pulled off their social media or from learning courses, internal and external, of them receiving awards, graduating or giving talks. These were put alongside recent footage and there were stark differences. The number one pointed to a young woman sat to her left and said that she was a forensic private investigator supplied by the home office and was the one who compiled all the footage and images. What? Home Office? Private Forensic Investigator? This must be serious. She claimed this 'evidence' she was providing was to illustrate she knew very well who the affected are and how there are more. She let us know internal investigations are still being carried out. She finished with several external bodies will be coming in and Parliament is drawing up a bill for punishments and furtherance around details she did not know. Back on A wing the officers were tense. The prisoners were moving about the office and officers that were in other locations on the wing like sharks. They seem to have a sixth sense when there is strife amongst staff and begin to conduct silent investigations to try to uncover what it could be and how they may exploit it. Some do it for something to do as they recently explained to me how boring it can be. Others do it for intelligence gathering.
Does business need to slow? Can new pipelines be constructed? Can supply be increased?
Does storage need to looked at? Are there any raids on the horizon?

*****

I had a week off after working nights and during that time I had probably spent more than
half my waking hours searching the life out of the internet for more information I gleaned
from that meeting with the governor. Before my leave I enquired lightly with staff and
prisoners and found out that the drug is called 'poxy' or Copoxydrate to give it its full name.
I saw in the meeting that there were around 3 prisoners on A wing that are in this scandal. I wanted to know why the governor was so angry and returning veiled threats like a powerful bback hand by Nadal whenever someone tried to speak up. I wanted to know why the staff, especially the older ones with the 'old school' attitude, seemed so tightly wound I thought
they were going to explode even if their best friend said "hello". I wanted to know what
exactly they did when they went steaming into a prisoner's cell, who was deemed a
problem, and they came out with a satisfied foul scowl which followed with me receiving a
command to "Just leave him there, 'Freshie!'" that is my new guy name that all my A wing
colleagues say with a little jolt of the neck, sarcastic emphasis and there eyes either bulge at
me or there is some kind of eye roll.
My search uncovered that Copoxydrate is what they call this decelerant of cognitive
facilities. The properties find and attach themselves to receptors in the region of the brain
that controls sensory perception and motor skills. It simultaneously keeps awareness

present but, depending on a dosage, slows the mind to experience time slower than the
outside world and shutting down the administered individuals motor skills. Trials were
originally expecting to help stroke sufferers. It was to be an Epi-pen style needle to be
administered by a carer at home during or as soon as it was realised a stroke had taken
place. The desired effect was to shut down motor skills to stop paralysis, slow the brain
firing at its usual rate to stop the wildfire like effect strokes have and proteins to help
rebuild any damage sustained to the brain. Trials seemed to show little results on mice but
the way it organised itself in the petri dish kept one 'pioneer' to press on and continue to
apply for more trials. They were granted a pig which seemed to show signs that there were
regenerative properties. The pig showed a renewed skill level as well as changes to
'cognitive facilitation', whatever that means. MRI scans were produced before a council of
renowned scientists as well as to the WHO. This was to provide the backdrop the 'pioneer',
Dr Sam Dryden PhD, needed to administer to the first human candidate. The volunteer, a
stroke patient, was injected with a micro dose. The time documented was 3 minutes 40
seconds when the volunteer, known as C-O-P 1, sprang out of her stupor like someone
coming up for air out of water. Dazed and gasping for breath she spoke at length of what
she got up to and seemed to think that "at least a year had passed by". Fast forward
through several more candidates, expanded to volunteers with a clean bill of health. These

trials all shown similar experiences of having an overwhelming perception of huge amounts of time passing by after only several actual minutes passing. Digging around didn't find much else on the clinical trials in terms of anything negative. Soon after Dr Dryden's name doesn't appear anymore in the more recent news articles. Instead, a new pharmaceutical company, BolenDuuko, seems to have taken over the production of the drug that 'saved the justice system'. This headline has many variants on different front pages of national tabloids and broadsheets accompanied with images of government officials shaking hands with an assortment of groups. People from BolenDuuko to people in the justice system.
Copoxydrate was pushed hard in parliament by both parties. Taglines that it will cut the prison population are rife. It was claimed that specific doses could be given in police stations or underneath the courtrooms in the holding cells after trials. The individual would experience the draining long haul of a prison sentence but could go back to work on Monday." It was rolled out but used sparingly at first. Phase 2 saw more than 50% of the courts ordering 'incarceration of the mind', these were primarily for those that were going to be serving no more than 12 months in prison. The prison population was cut over a 10-month period to an all-time low not seen in decades. Prisons were declared safe as crowding dwindled. Most prisons were directed to move to single cell occupancy on all wings. The experience was said to not be a pleasant one. Interviews and a timeline were documented

and compiled from what was made available from C-0-P 1 to the latest 'cognitively released' prisoner. Reports from think tanks and other social rights groups detail that the experience is slightly different for each individual but there are elements that remain the same. Night terrors interspersed with the framework of living daily life whilst incarcerated mentally. The daily life aspect has caused scientists to step in to say that it is similar to dreaming.
Dreaming of people, places, incidents etc. are all creations of the mind that they have been to, met or been involved in. The civil and social rights groups say that this doesn't explain the moving on of time and the advancements in society that these individuals describe. No further comment has been made on this.
My investigation uncovered that crime reduced as people were becoming increasingly frightened of the use of Copoxydrate. There were more and more online videos being liked, shared and commented on the video sharing platform, SnoopViews. These videos showed lifelong criminals that have graced the same court rooms and many a prison with their presence in this great land who did not want another shot of Copoxydrate. The individuals are screaming they do not want it, are resisting security and begging the judge to change their sentencing. These videos regularly show the criminals trying to bargain for extra years serving physical time instead of the 'poxy' jab. The human rights groups, both national and international have pressed that this is inhumane. The argument being that the 'condemned'

mind is aging at an accelerated rate compared to the rest of the body. "Too little evidence, research and findings prove concrete benefits or harm at this time", was the response in both written and televised interviews by the government. The facts that the mainstream news is running with are; crime is down and so is re-offending. The drug is for the discretion of the judge but it is said that the Copoxydrate route is preferred by the Home Office and justice system over the traditional 'physical imprisonment', as it is now known. This is due to the marked drop in crime. Re-offending is 38% lower on the previous year with overall crime down by 21%. Both numbers, it is claimed, rise after each injection as the longest sentenced passed was 10 years which took, by the newly formed, Scientific Council for Justice, less than 36 hours. Wow! More recent news articles read that the length of time is distorted as they have tweaked the formula from the initial C-0-P 1 findings. This is due to the new direction they realised that they could take with the new results. It was claimed that the original broke down quickly and that is why the formula changed. The shady side is that the ingredients aren't fully disclosed as they have been put in the classified section of British law. This, it is claimed, is to stop it being used on dissidents and opponents in countries that have little to no human rights observations. That is the premise for the creation of the Scientific Council for Justice, or the SCJ, which only 15% are scientists. This has poured more fuel on the fire as conspiracy theorists' question why all aren't named and why heads from different sectors of the military and the private military industrial complex supremos are on the board. Questions around particular mental disorders and the mixing of other prescribed and illegal drugs and their impact on the length of time the 'condemned' are under. No official lasting effects have been proven, mainly due to no test being carried out after the 'resurfacing'. Friends and family of the condemned have set up groups on social media and have had some time on air pleading with the government to stop Copoxydrate administration. Here the trail goes flat and there is no mention of the prison system. Note to self, time to switch from operation 'get to know the prisoners' to operation 'find out what the fuck is going on.'

*****

Several days back and I had been given a little respect, and I mean 'a little.' They stopped calling me 'freshie' but rarely called me by my name. I think to my colleagues I balanced A wing out to the higher ups as I didn't have the 'old school' attitude. This little respect allowed me to ask more questions regarding the meeting and the prisoners that were mentioned. I didn't have the courage to ask outright but I did it under a veil of disdain towards the governor and how she behaved towards us in 'that' meeting and resentment towards the prisoner. This is what I uncovered. I couldn't get a handle on when it started to

be used in here but the entire prison system received vast quantities of Copoxydrate. This was for safe storage as the army bases and regular compounds were full due to 'exponential development and breakthroughs in several areas ranging from pharmaceuticals to weaponry. This was decided after the government stated that Copoxydrate was a success on several breakfast news channels and held a daily briefing. The go ahead was given for the prisons to administer it on some prisoners who could be freed after serving the rest of their physical time through 'cognitive housing'. This is how almost all the prisons could move to single cell occupancy, meaning less prisoners which meant less work for prison officers.
Violence reduced with the population. The Consort of Prison Custodians, CPC, rallied fiercely as it looked as if prisons could be done away with altogether. This prompted sparse use of Copoxydrate on the inside of prisons. Self-preservation. Instead of using it to free prisoners, it was used as a punishment. Instead of 36 hours in the segregation unit, you would get rough housed then get an unspecified amount of the drug pumped in you by an untrained officer. They would be out for a couple hours but within their own mind decades had passed. That is by the calculations from the C-0-P 1 trials. Research hasn't been done to see how it reacts with a depressant or stimulant that is already in the system. The stories I pieced together were startling. Now I see why the governor was upset but there was something else that wasn't being said. Have things been happening in other prisons? What

about the Parliamentary Bill she spoke of? Who or what would be affected? There was no mention of any of this on the news. I was baffled and slightly worried. What am I involved in?
With all this new information I couldn't believe that I had missed it when it was happening right in front of my eyes. The storming of cells. The zonked-out prisoner all cut and bruised.
The dramatic weight loss. The sudden and immediate change in behaviour. Warning me away. How did I not click on? Crazy. Looking with opened eyes I watched the 'problem' prisoners. There were 3 'problems', as they were referred to as, that were of note. 2 acted the same and one was in a league of his own. Others had been jabbed up a couple of times but they seemed to have 'learned their lesson' and turned their lives around and were doing away with distance learning course at an extremely fast pace as well as reading copious amounts of books from the library. These, O'Brian and that referred to as 'The Learners' as they were into education and had learnt the lesson that he wanted them to with his punishments. Remembering how they were before all this scandal happened. The life and vibrancy, the one O'Brian and that refer to as 'problem no 1' was a man mountain before all this. Within days he was as thin as a rake. What drugs did I think did this? He wandered the landings looking no further than 1 metre in front of him but about 1000m down. The stare was penetrating. The unnerving thing was that his eyes never moved. It was as if his retinas

had been disconnected. He never blinked either. The other 2 'problems' were said to speak
gibberish and behaved as if they were completely separate to the rest of us on the wing.
They move erratically in their own personal space. There facial expressions do not falter or
flicker with any type of emotion. They were boisterous lads, obviously as that is why they
were subdued physically and then cognitively by O'Brian and his lot, but they now were
reclusive, spent most of their time in a hunched squat facing the walls. They were popular
and by far nowhere near the bottom of the pecking order but now they recoiled as if in pain
or behaved in a 'Rain-man' type way if any of their old counterparts went anywhere near
them. They simply failed to recognise them. After several attempts they were written off
and left alone. One I'm not too sure what he was saying but the other was speaking a kind
of Sino-Russo hybrid. I'm a film buff and watched plenty subtitled films to catch the odd
word when it reoccurs. I have a penchant for language and dialects. I asked the officers if
there were any notes or instances where he had spoken any other language before. They all
bent over laughing. He was known intimately by Her Majesty's custodians as he had been
coming from a young age. They said he can't even pass the entry level 3 basic skills courses
the prisoners are forced to take. So how? Where was this learnt? How does someone learn
two languages and then create a hybrid?
My investigations hadn't stopped but were on pause. Since I started I had been put on duty

to record all the incidents that occurred on A wing.
There were power outages regularly.
Cracks had appeared in the brick work on this wing as well as the nearest wings and closest
perimeter wall. These had been attributed to the low rumbling earthquakes that I logged as
the cause for the fractures in structure. I had to do wing inspections and cell inspections
more regularly as earthquakes were increasing which produced more cracks and widened
old ones. This seemed to worry O'Brian and the rest of his officers, but I didn't know why.
The news was acknowledging the quakes which eased my mind but seemed to make the
others tenser.

*****

There was some excitement one week when there was an empty prison cell. During the
nightly roll check. Officers checked and re-checked all the cells on A wing. They checked the
showers, laundry room, storeroom and even our office. They re-opened the cell and had a
look around. O'Brian was on leave so the rest of the group combined make up about 75% of
the nastiness, strength and sadism that O'Brian brings in one singular man. They were
hurling abuse in the blatantly empty cell. There were threats of harm and a 'Poxy' jab if he
didn't come out. They checked the locks and bars, which were all still intact. They refused to
call it in as this cell belonged to the fast becoming infamous 'problem no 1'. This prisoner

has been given copious amounts of Copoxydrate in terms of separate jabs and fullness of the needles barrel. He is on medication for mental illness as well as being known to dabble in ones of A wings black market. I can only surmise and wince that this particular prisoner has had 100s upon 100s of years experiencing a full vivid picture of his life and daily routines whilst being 'mentally incarcerated'. Radios were snapping with a repeated need for the confirmation of A wings prisoner count. It was a group decision, I wasn't asked, to say the full capacity numbers and to let the night clockies pick up on it either through the night or at the 6am roll count. Blame was to be placed at their feet. At this part of the decision all glared at me to ensure I was on board. I concurred.

Arriving at work, I was braced in the morning meeting to become embroiled in my own personal scandal in regard to the wider Copoxydrate abuse scandal. To my astonishment there was no mention of it. We all kind of slyly looked at each other but all maintained our poise and filtered out at the end of the meeting and went to A wing without saying a word.

We entered the wing and began unlocking the prisoners. All were looking at the officer getting closer and closer to Problem no 1's cell. He finally reached the door, flicked up the observation flap and just stood there for what seemed like an eternity. We all stalled in our tracks for several moments until he unlocked the door and moved on. The door opened fully and out he emerged. Eyes glued to his 1 metre point, 1000m depth stare and shuffled along the landing. What? How?

I was accosted by an officer as I was updating the incident sheet after my routine cell/wing checks. The conversation was that I better not have placed the half missing prisoner in with the other incidents. I assured I had not and there were all the weeks' forms in the 'out' tray to be checked as they are submitted to the business hub once weekly.

*****

One incident that definitely had to be placed in the incident report forms was absolutely incredible, during the morning cell checks a massively shared phenomenon was experienced. I was just toddling through cells tapping bars and pressing alarms to ensure there weren't any loose bars or cut throughs and that the prisoners in-cell alarm worked in case of emergency. I was just exiting a cell when all of a sudden, from the corner of my eye, I saw prisoners on all four landings closest to the main gate begin to go down. It was like a choreographed Mexican wave of sorts, but they stayed down trembling and grunting. The phenomenon was moving towards me. I saw officers go down that do not partake in anything that the prisoners do which made me think this isn't a game. Lights popped.
Finally, I was struck. I can only liken the 'grip' as a whole-body vibration not too unlike the one felt in your hands from a games console controller. Then I started to become lightheaded.
It felt as if my blood was being forced down into my lower extremities, blood

pooling in my fingers and toes. Then It was like my knees had magnets in them as one buckled to the floor as if attracted to it. A hand followed, the other knee, another hand. My spine! Oh gosh my spine. I was struggling to breathe. Instinctively I was trying to stand. I could hear the sky lights buckle, crack and begin to shower down on all of us. The glass was as fine as sugar. The pressure took me down to one elbow. Someone shuffled towards me. My teeth were gritted. Eyes bulging. Doors moaned and creaked. Railings groaned. My shoulder on my elbowed side hit the ground and I rolled over. Hands pinned to the ground shoulder high. My eyes were being forced back up into my head. As they rolled up I made eye contact, for the very first time since I'd been on the wing, with Problem no 1. Darkness. Serenity.

*****

'Gravity forcing us down or the earth pulling us down' was what I wrote in the incident report. I was told by the other officers to leave out that I saw Problem no 1 walking around as normal not affected in the slightest. All three problems were found in their cells. I just so happened to be 2 doors away from Problem no 1's cell at the time of the incident. They were all found in their cells when the alarm bell was sounded from the control room as the security team eventually saw camera screens out and everyone on their hands, knees, stomachs and backs with posters and noticeboards all on the floor. They watched until the

cameras furthest from the main gate went black. We were all in an exhausted state or
completely unconscious. Those closest to me in all directions were unconscious. Security
thought it was a riot until they saw everyone out of action. The suspected rioters, the ones
already identified as having possible mutinous inclinations were just as worse for wear as
the officers. A mild effect was felt in other parts of the prison. A wing seeming to be the
epicentre and those closest got a heavier dose.
It took several days for all of us to get our bearings. This just so happened when an external
team came in to investigate what had be happening with the Copoxydrate abuse. I can't
particularly recall what they did when they were elsewhere in the prison. I can't recall what
they did when they came on to A wing. I can't even recall what was said during my
interview. I was told from others that they were taking blood samples and have took all the
CCTV footage and paperwork. The official story was that these were government officials
but there were rumours, from the prisoners that they were actually from the Scientific
Council for Justice. I don't know why I found this surprising that this could come from a
prisoner as that is where I have found most food for thought whilst working here. I fed this
back to O'Brian and the others and they leaned hard to that inclination. They started to take
the stance that these can't do anything to them. The next day they had some mean military
looking guys in suits and glasses with them.

*****

Walking down the courtroom steps for the last time was, although an eye-opening experience, somewhat anti-climactic. Justice had been served as O'Brian and his cronies all received life sentences for the mistreatment and abuse of some of the prisoners by use of Copoxydrate. I was never really in the picture and didn't really have to give evidence or be a
witness as CCTV showed I was an outsider to O'Brian's inner circle as well as statements
given by some of the prisoners. All our home personal computers, phones, tablets and
personal laptops were seized and mine showed I looked into Copoxydrate after 'that
meeting' and my story was backed with my odd little flutter on the Inside Watch and the
Whistler Award websites. On the other hand, the evidence on O'Brian and the rest of my A
wing colleagues was overwhelming. They had CCTV, bodycam footage, prisoner statements,
comments from the governors and their personal technology. I was relieved from duties
whilst all this was pending but I was told that it is a formality and I can return the Monday
after the trial finishes. If I want. The 'victims', as the prisoners abused with Copoxydrate
were so called in court, whereabouts were unknown as they had simply vanished. Details
from that were not entered in the case against the officers which I found totally strange.
The bill had been passed by parliament it seems to silence anyone from speaking out. The
Copoxydrate was removed from the prison estate and is rumoured to have been buried until
further, suitable, storage space is found.

*****

I hadn't been able to sleep properly since the 'gravity' incident. There was no mention of that on the news or in the courtroom. The external investigators were aware of this and still nothing. Who were they? One night I awoke during the night and I swear 'problem no. 1' was stood at the foot of my bed. Staring directly at me. I'm not sure if it actually happened. I had a tremendous back log of nights where I lacked sleep. It could have been the 11-week trial where we saw footage and images of the 'victims' that played on my mind too. He just stood at the bottom of my bed mouthing something. A voice in my head did slowly crescendo in the correct rhythm of the mouthing. It just said over and over, "I am Carruthers."

*****

A phone rings.
Man: "Hello."
Woman 1: "He's in possession."
Man: "Good. You know what to do".
Hangs up.
Dial tone.
Numbers keyed.
Ring ring. Ring ring.
Woman 2: "Hello."
*****
Woman 1: "Initiate Human Transcendent Creation Programme."
Woman 2: "Yes maam."
Line goes dead

The End

Statements on Disappearances

Individuals involved

- HTS – 1 (Nominal 1)
- LTS – 1
- LTS – 2

Officers

- 101
- 102
- 103
- 104

Summary

The disappearances were 3 separate incidents.

LTS – 1's disappearance

OFFICER 101
0917 hours - LTS – 1 shuffled up to the officer on the gate who was guarding whilst simultaneously ticking off the relevant inmates going to work. As he neared the officer 101, who noticed him several inmates back in the queue, he thought he's in no state to work but checked the list anyway to confirm he is not needed off the wing anywhere. **CCTV footage backs this statement**. Once he confirmed this he shouted another officer to escort LTS -1 back to his cell as he is aware of the "'poxy' stuff".

OFFICER 102
0918 hours - On the way to LTS – 1's cell the officer 102 was speaking to him. The officer kept glancing at LTS – 1 as they were walking side by side. She noticed that his skin started to change, as a chameleon would, as he passed doors, walls and notice boards. The officer was adamant as LTS – 1 was shuffling slow so the changes were slow. She remembers that it was getting increasingly more difficult to see him. Shocked and trying to tame her adrenaline rush she tried to grab hold of his wrist, to which she says all she had was the thought to raise her hand when LTS – 1's head bolted straight up and round to face her, making intense eye contact. She felt the vibration just like the 'gravity' incident but it was only strong enough to root her to the ground and not be able to raise he arms. She felt contained. By now all she could see were his eyes as he totally blended in to the background. He slipped out of his dressing gown and closed his eyes. She collapsed. **CCTV footage backs this statement.** By the time she came around in a hospital bed, 1348 hours, all 3 had disappeared.

FORENSIC INVESTIGASTOR
The strange thing picked up on the cameras were that no one seemed to notice the officer down. People walked round and even over her. When questioned about this, the prisoners claimed that they did not know she was there. Visual observations back this up as there seemed to be a total obliviousness to her until after HTS – 1 left.

LTS – 2's disappearance

OFFICER 103
1332 hours – Officer 103 went to unlock LTS – 2's cell for afternoon association to find that the cell was empty.

HTS – 1's disappearance

OFFICER 104
1334 hours – Officer 104 went to unlock HTS – 1's cell when the door folded into oblivion right in front of his eyes. HTS - 1 was stood staring directly at him, feet slightly off the ground. Officer 104 claims that
HTS – 1 then just started to fall apart from the outer edges to the core. He likened it to blowing sand or something grainy except it disappeared. Then he was gone. He complains of piercing headaches since incident.

FOR INTERNAL USE ONLY

Incident Reports

Evidence

- Wing CCTV
- Body cam footage

Summary

A full observation has been given to the whole footage made available to us. We found the wing CCTV to be the most useful. The incidents that were reported by Officer 108 on Form – 501 gave us the most direction in which to take this investigation. We were able to look at the footage that is nearest time stamped with the incident report. We were able to see that the HTS (Higher Transcendent Subject) and both LTS's (Lower Transcendent Subject) were on each other's vicinities at the time of the 'phenomena' happening. The individuals just so happened to live in different areas on the wing but when they passed by each other, whether side by side or one on the landing above the other, that is when 'phenomena' happened such as fractures in the infrastructure and power outages. The greatest incident of all was the then labelled 'gravity' incident. This has been viewed from multiple angles a before the cameras went down. We were able to see that the individuals were all gathered by our teams so that they could be interviewed without any interference from wing staff or prisoners. When our team gathered these in the room, it is said a low rumbling started as they were getting nearer each other. The next thing they knew is the 'gravity' incident which is documented. Our team awoke with the Riot Squad around them, minus HTS – 1 and LTS - 1 and 2.

Conclusion

There appears to be a significant field or aura around the Transcendents that triggers when they are together. We are unsure what the true implications are but we believe there to be a correlation between the 'gravity' event and the disappearance. Officers stated that between the 'gravity' event and the disappearances, there seemed to be a slight edge back towards their original selves. This leads us to believe that they reached another level within themselves. We are unsure how this looks for the world but we fear this could be out of our hands.

Plan of action

Programmes have been given the go ahead to create someone to be controlled by us and can locate and capture the Transcendents.

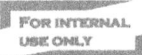

FOR PUBLIC USE ONLY

Report Findings of [redacted] Human [redacted] CHT – 1 (redacted)

Test subject Name: [redacted] O'B[redacted] known as (CHT - 1)

Age: 57

Blood type: [redacted]

Plan of Action:

- Micro-dose with Copoxydrate
- Use verbal suggestion throughout [redacted] theta state [redacted]

Summary:

- 'Resurfacing' shows signs of [redacted]
- CHT – 1 is going through [redacted] appearance
- CHT – 1 [redacted] resuscitated [redacted] needed [redacted]reatment

FOR PUBLIC USE ONLY

Report Findings on HTS - 1 (redacted)

Name of subject: [redacted]Carruthers, known as HTS - 1

Date: [redacted]

Body age (in years): 40

Cognitive age (in years):[redacted]

Blood type:[redacted] (new classification)

Time mentally incarcerated: [redacted]

Suggested abilities;

- [redacted]
- Regenerative [redacted]
- [redacted] (fountain of youth theory)
- Skin [redacted]
- [redacted]
- [redacted] to and from global positions
- [redacted] reading
- Copoxydrate in [redacted] ready to [redacted] at will
- Move through [redacted]
- [redacted] (doesn't necessarily need to eat)
- [redacted]

Rate injected: [redacted]

Cc used:[redacted]

Summary:

HTS – 1 is one of a kind. HTS – 1 seems to have [redacted] no end. We cannot [redacted] HTS – 1 may have [redacted] and with his [redacted]. This type of [redacted] totally unexpected. HTS - 1 [redacted]. All the [redacted] elevate [redacted] **together**. This is of great concern. Steps to [redacted] is in the process. Expected rate of success is [redacted]

POEMS

The SAS say 'who dares wins'
GAS man say 'who stares wins'
Facilitators, therapists and counsellors say 'who bares wins'
But when it comes to loved ones 'who cares wins'
My life's been talk joke and smoke
My life's been doe over hoes
My life's been so over board
That I thought road was home
Why?
Media and a tedious life
Media feedin ya lies
Surrounded by evil and serious guys
Dat are in deeper den seas and their tides
And I concurred so I was conquered
Been nefarious to be wanted
Now I'm in a cell alone
Selling sombre

*****

Sincere warmth, security and connectedness,
The untangler of knots
Shelter from the storm
Life giver
The oompf in my step
The swell in my chest
The knowing where I'm going
The sun in the sky
The sustenance to maintain
Bearer of brunt's
Comforter
Patient and content
The misser
The missing
The missed
My .... missus

*****

The yoga pose I hold
Doesn't just allow movement in the joint,
It crates free space in my mind at certain points,
The yoga pose I hold,
Doesn't just lengthen the muscle
It strengthens the muscle,
Tension and struggle means its working,
relieves physical and mental burdens,
and when in da sentence I struggle,
A yoga pose I hold,
Ascension so subtle,
from I hold a yoga pose,
life scripts change
a new story does unfold
calmness

*****

I have started meditating to clear my mind,
In controlled silence,
Colours and clarity arise,
Enveloped by,
Soothing sensations that emanate from my spine, I feel so light,
I feel so high,
I feel I can rewind and fast forward time
Or stay supremely in the moment,
When the mind is quiet, reality is real

*****

When I jacked him, was funny,
When I jabbed him, showed courage,
When I stabbed him, was worried,
2nd strike life, feel buried
A judge, judged me on a judgement I made,
Adrenaline rush, thrusted, ribs cushioned the blade,
Dint give fuck, fuck him, put in his place,
Good blows, blood soaked, a dozen mistakes,

*****

You may have seen my lows,
but you ant seen my zenith, apex, peaks, tops and highs,
Your eyes, spy with surprise, something that lies, within me
that rises up to the sky,
and far beyond stars that light the night,
My talents and ability,
My balance and agility,
Allow me to challenge the rigidity,
of life,
& manage it infinite

*****

Man on da **wing**

There's man on da wing dat are shit faced
There's man on da wing with a big case
There's man on da wing with big waist
There's man on da wing with pure rib cage
There's man on da wing getting big gains
There's man on da wing with sick game
There's man on da wing with spliff bait
There's man on da wing with big chains
There's man on da wing who say mix raced
No fellah it's mixed race
There's man on da wing dat rip mates
There's man on da wing dat shift weight
There's man on da wing who don't think they should be here
and it is all just one big mistake
There's man on da wing dat get blanked ca you can't listen
to what dat prick says
There's man on da wing dat dig grave
only their own
There's man on da wing whose wrist gape
ca nobody listens

There's man on da wing who produce click bait
There's man on da wing kicking off ca their scripts late
Incoming or outgoing
There's man on da wing dat snitch mate
dats a risk mate an ya gambling with big stakes

*****

I grew up with snuggles
Love yous and jumped in puddles
Played dalavio, bulldog and got into tussles
And when I smelt alcohol I should go to
My room cuz I'm not getting no cuddles
I must say that this left me puzzled
For years
Which left me open to the roads
As my mind was malleable and supple
I was getting in deep without a shovel
I was livin in my own little bubble
Pain an gashes on my knuckles
Gettin into trouble
With the law
Roads are rough you may get pummelled
And kids, teens, adults and OAPs will say 'fuck you'
My names takin off like a shuttle
I was a star looked on by Hubble
Embedded deeply is the struggle
Under dat weight I nearly buckled
Man int a clown but I juggled
Deez roads are mix up, all a muddle
Gyally love me with da stubble
An cuz I hustle and got muscle
I had to do a spell in jail but I'm a muggle
Bed rock hard like Barney Rubble's
So I pray after I do ghusl

*****

I'm sick of dis food
I'm sick of deez screws

I’m sicka deez dudes
who are thicker den 2
Planks of wood
They get karate chopped
I don't wanna hear how hard he woz
Or how he partied lots
Or how many cars he's got
Or yards he’s got
I don't believe da guy
I don't wanna demonise
But he must think I'm bleary eyed
An can't see his lies
When we talk about needin doe he tops it off
Like a pizza pie
But den he's released
Months have passed it's been a few
Den one random day we see da news
It’s da same guy dat we knew
Yeah dat guy with stories in his too baggy prison trousers
Dey showed us his boat, his money, his houses,
Sentenced in his absence as he's out still
He had over da police, customs and council
An dats why you shouldn't judge

*****

In da ends/thinkin'

I was in da ends with some sinners,
I was in da ends with da rillest,
I was in da ends with guerrillas,
I was in da ends with people that turned out to be killers,
I was in da ends with leaders,
I was in da ends with dealers,
I was in da ends with man dat will pull up and beat ya,

Lately I've been thinking' of business plans,

Thinking of writin' to places who give out grants,
Thinkin' of getting da ends on a fitness stance,
Thinking of being a role model and helpin' prison mans,
I'm not da same man from da olden days,
Paroles comin' up and I'm golden mate,
Don't care what the old soldiers say,
Ca in da last 10 years I've served over 8,

I'm **done**
I'm **thinkin' of change!**

*****

Moons

Sentenced to 772 moons,
I'm not one to stress or stew,
I'm still gunna bun a lil bit of dat self-soothe,
And keep hold of dem heavy duty bags in case of a jail or cell move,

Deh pan road again, I'm back!
In life I'm in da red, I need to get in da black,
Knife crime my lifeline and I'll attack,
600 moons is all I could last,

2nd strike,
"weapon?" "knife",
"you could've let 'em slide,"
"it dunt work like dat in my dishevelled mind,"

I was a callous baddie, charismatic and embarrassed easy,
Now I'm empathic, solution based, use my voice, make good choices and de-escalate,
My new path is productive and its da one I choose,
It's been an enlightenin' 2038 moon!

*****

My favourite film

My favourite film used to be Scarface,
Cuz I felt like I could relate,
Rags 2 riches,
Takeover cities,
And seriously gettin' paid,

I got feedback for a long time,
And saw where I was going wrong in life,
I became more emotionally balanced,
And now I feel alive and look for positive challenge,

My life is easy, care free and fun,
Solution based, I action plan any of life's bumps,
I set goals to achieve and I get it done,
That's why my new favourite film is Forest Gump

Inspirational, Jen-nay!

****

If I was ...

If I was ...
... free,
I would show L-O-V-E,
To my missis,
Shower her with kisses,
Real life emoji, smilin' devilish,
Talk about our future and reminisce,

If I was ...
... rich,

I'd make sure I covered all da loved one's basics,
Raise da disadvantaged's game, so we're on da same pitch,

Give a helpin' hand,
I've so many unselfish plans,

If I was ...
... a poet,
I'd put my heart down on da page,
Twist and turn like I'm in a maze,
Find myself, be unafraid,
Say what I say to keep me sane,
Trust those I share with to keep it **SAFE.**

*****

Love

Love is the ethereal **ocean** to all. You choose how deep you go. Do you stay in the shallows?
Or dive deep? Head over heels? It is all encompassing but cannot be seen. It cannot be touched but
is felt. Love can be gracious, unconditional, intoxicating and leave us uplifted and feeling high. Love can
be dangerous. A lion with a thorn in its paw. If love is 'done right' its like everlasting rays of

sunlight that provides nourishment to the parts we lack or do/did not know we had.

We can mimic the **cosmos.** We can revolve around what is important. We can light the

path in the dark. We can be a guiding **star.** We can be attracted to each other. We can collide.We can be lonely,

desolate and barren. We can be **wordly.** Distant

and cold or too close and if things get heated. We can pull people down to the ground. We can be too high and take their air. We can produce life. We can die out.
We can change the tides, ebb and flow. We can change like the wind. We can be on shaky ground. We can destroy homes.
Love is all this. Talk about your feelings. Grow your best bits. Just. Love.

*****

Do you know what I mean?

Days in ya sentence when you just wanna sleep an' sleep,
Juhnartameen?
Ca its easier to just get ya head down ca you can *control* ya dreams,
Juhnartameen?
When ya watchin' a screw get on to a prisoner just cuz he dunt like him,
Juhnartameen?
And you can see the prisoner just wants to take off his chin,
Juhnartameen?

Can't take the food no more so you just whip some fish sutten in da microwave,
Juhnartameen?
Need dat parole date so you know you can eat summet nourishing, dat'll be da day,
Juhnartameen,

Dem days when ya full of energy, could run a marathon or climb mount Everest,
Juhnartameen?
But ya stuck in a cell, hell, yells and bells,
Juhnartameen?

Dem days when ya just sorry for what you did but nobody cares?

There's a window 8ft high so you can't even stare
Out of it to clear ya mind,
see summet nice
or help with da passin' of time,
Juhnartamenn?

Dem ones der when dey've got ya by da balls with der carrot and stick?
Threatnin' dis or dat, tit for tats,
Cuz dey're inept and don't wanna be held responsible?
Juhnartameen?

Ders no meaning or purpose so,
People act kiddie, divvy, giddy, get lippy or damage,
End up in da block or on basic for excess energy they couldn't manage,
There's no art classes or Spanish,
No mechanics, just drill in some good positive habits man,

Juhnartameen?

Rant over=)

*****

It means something/thank you

Writing in to a competition,
Winning, being recognised and acknowledged,
Means something,
Being offered help
to better oneself,
Mentored in something that is centred,
Around the individual,
It means something,
Placing contents of the mind,
On Instagram to be admired,
Fans the flames and stokes the fire,
Means something,
Mind, heart, aura, self-esteem,

Confidence, all grow,
Ten feet tall,
From summet so small
as a letter,
It means something, thank you
I appreciate appreciation,
And appreciate those who appreciate,
cuz it elevates
the soul and spirit,
And spurs me to say ....

... thank you ...

You mean something!

Keep it up!

5 minutes

The summer breeze lightly grazing his face. A light glistening of sweat on his brow. He brings the cigarette he is holding in his left hand to his lips. He takes a deep drag. His cheeks sink. The skin around his neck tightens. The end flares up and races towards the cork. The smoke in his mouth, passes his pharynx, passes his larynx, through his trachea and swirls in his bronchus and alveoli. He exhales through his nose. He is comfortable and content as he walks down the street on this nice, hot day. On his mind is a Nourishment. A quick liquid breakfast before he goes to see a friend to acquire a bag of stress relief. He has a glance at his watch and sees it is 12:17pm. Between draws on his cigarette he can smell freshly cut grass. The smell triggers multiple memories. Memories with his grandad, memories playing football, memories of playing hide and seek with family and friends on his estate. Sounds of children playing nearby float through the air along with the changing music as he walks by houses and passing cars. Bob Marley, Rag n Bone Man, Rihanna, UB40 and Yung Bxne is leaking down on to the street from open windows and doors. The summer breeze lightly washes over him again. Someone shouts him from further up the street. He shields his eyes from the sun with his right hand, takes another drag with his left as he tries to make out who it is. He recognises him and holds his right hand up high and smiles, "Yes, my bruddah!" he replies and keeps stepping. Squinting from the blazing sun, as well as reflections off parked cars and light-coloured paving slabs. The plan today is to smoke, chill and tan.

Simple. His phone vibrates in his pocket against his right leg. He fumbles in his grey joggers
and sees it is an ex. Not today he thinks and red phones her. He knows a text and WhatsApp
ping will arrive shortly. He sees the summer breeze approach this time as a crisp packet
comes to life and slowly glides across the tarmac. The breeze hits him. Enters his t-shirt,
makes a quick route around him and exits out the fabric. It felt good. The trees lining the
pavement seem to give him a little nod in the breeze. He crosses the road, a car he doesn't
recognise turns the corner in front of him. It slows suddenly and does a U-turn. He thinks
'opps' as he couldn't see into it due to the glare from the sun. He knows he is quick so
decides to give them a little time to show their hand. The windows roll down and it's all
familiar faces. "Yo my G." says the rear passenger.
"Sayin yo?" the front passenger nods as he says this unsmiling.
"Fuck all, going shop. What you man on wi?". The rear passenger motions for him to get in
by opening the door. He jumps in. Touches everyone's fist. He asked what they are all doing
and where did the car come from. "Don't worry 'bout that, bro" says the rear passenger
who has turned to face him with one leg up on the seat. "Eyar! I'm only going to dat shop
der!" he exclaims as the car takes a quick left. No seatbelt on, he almost slides into the man
next to him. "Look. Dem man are out in a small number on Collegiate. Quick drill and we'll
drop you back at da shop like the nanan you are." The car exploded with laughter at his expense.
Except him. He knows he can't refuse as they backed him up when 'dem man', 'opps',

whatever, jumped him. "I'm in a tee, tatts out an' everyting. How can I crash like this?" he holds out his arms to illustrate his point. "No mask, no nuttin'. Dis is bait. Fully".
"Don't watch dat famble." At that the rear passenger smiled as he turned and put his hand under the parcel shelf. Every time his hand reappeared it produced something. First a hoody. Then a black bandanna. Finally, a slim, long, serrated edged, bread knife. His leg and the side of his face tingled at the site of it as it was the same type of blade that was used on him in the aforementioned spots. His heart beat quickened. His pupils dilate as he throws on the hoody. He finds himself drift towards 'that' part of his mind. Beast mode kicks in an he is primed for violence. Fuck da world and everyone in it. There's no back stepping. No guts, no glory. After the 'glide' he knows he will have the most euphoric feeling course through his being. He will swear that his ancestors will feel it. His rep will be enhanced and he will have further doors opened up to him. The ladies' situation will also elevate. He knows they love a bad boy. The badder the better.
This thought flashes through his mind for a second. Track 2 'Teddy Brukshot 2' on Loski's album, A Drill Story, plays in the background. He grabs the handle above the door and stares at that spot out the window that makes the outside scenery of houses, flats, trees and streetlights roll past in a left dripping wash as if a freshly painted painting has been left on its side to run. He looks at his watch. 12: 18 pm. He catches some of what's being said.
"You know how we do doe, no man can try a ting an get away with it." Says the rear

passenger animatedly. "This is a collision course. We are gonna crash on deez man hard. Ya get meh!" He watches the rear passenger grab the shoulder of the front seat passenger who is in front of him an says "We are gonna do dis together yeah." The rear passenger then turns to him and says the same thing but dragged out the final syllable of together. It was uncharacteristic. He knew they were close. He could feel his pulse in his neck and fingertips. This was normal for him. The music was turned up louder to gas man. He has done this many time over many years. He was scared when they did this the first few times, but when you walk away unscathed and have more of a name for yourself then before you left it is intoxicating. He was at his highest heights in terms of status, money and, currently, adrenaline. The others were jamming to the song, and describing what they were going to do to 'dem man' in detail. The bandanna was uncomfortable on his face as he was hot in the car with the big hoody on. There was a musty smell coming from the bandanna too. They turned the music up even higher. The noise reverberated through the car. Hitting his ear drums and penetrating, once again, to the memory zones of his brain. This time he sees nights out, his bredrins, sexy gyal, good vibes and being respected by others outside the circle and out da ends. It feels good and a slight calmness emanates for a second. "We're here." Says the rear passenger with barely tamed excitement as he pulls his bally down.

"They ant seen us" the front passenger states, somewhat muffled behind his bandanna, with slight emotion as he adjusts.

"Slow down" the rear passenger is now sat almost centrally in the back leaning into the front
for a better look. "Turn dat down an' pull behind dat car." is the rear passenger command.
"Where are da others?" said the driver quite antsy.
"They shunt be long. They've just gone to get the whammy." Barks the rear passenger.
"How many's there?" The rear passenger was giddy. He lives for this stuff. Beyond excited
for the carnage and mayhem that is about to ensue. "Der int many." Is the reply from the
front passenger.
"Alright, fuck it. Come." The rear passenger exited the car and the others followed. Creeping
behind the cars that lined the pavement towards the kill zone adrenaline flooded in to them
all. Eyes wide. Body primed. Nearing the enemy position were another, much larger, group. They were hidden behind a privit in a garden across the road as there was a party going on
for one of them. Outnumbered and they've seen them. 4 lads trapped between 6 on one
side and 18 on the other. "Opppppsssss!!" All hell broke loose. Shouting, swearing, glasses
smashing. Hood pulled over his head. Blows pepper his body. Several of the blows leave him
extremely breathless. He thinks 'this is new'. He swings with abandon the blade in his own
hand. He is bent over. Head forced down by the hand that has his hood. He knew him and
his assailants had moved from one side of the road to the other. Very swiftly. He was pinned
between a car and as his heads was being controlled and held down, there were sparse
moments when he should see. Similar to an eclipse he had to be watching for when the
hood, palm or bandanna was not aligned he could make out several pairs of trainers that

were facing him. They were darting around. Side to side. Back and forth. Always angling in and out to get the better of him and rain down as many blows without being can't in the process. Seeing or not made no difference. He gained no advantage. He was inflicting heavy damage and he knew it. Eventually there was a POP! POP! POP! The cavalry had arrived. The opps scattered. One let out a groan, hit the deck, got back to his feet and hopped off as fast as he could. The rear passenger was slightly injured and made his way back to the car when he realised one was missing. He ran back to see him in a mess. The bandanna that he had given him was up his face, covered in blood. He was gasping. His eyes wide. Fear in them. All he wanted to do was chill, smoke and tan. The rear passenger sat in the blood on his knees, cradling his friends head. Knife wounds everywhere. He pulls the bandanna off him. As he does this the injured man catches sight of the rear passengers watch. 12:21pm. The car they came in pulls up at the rear passenger's side. The engine is being rev'd savagely. He gets in. They screech off. Together yeah? Right. Alone, the breeze pushes plastic cups and other debris up towards him. He does not feel a thing, just cold. But not a cold at skin level. It is a deep penetrating cold. Emanating from somewhere deep within outwards. The type felt when you touch a concrete slab or gravestone. Even in summer it is still such a cold that cannot be rested on for too long as the cold is too intense. He knew he was jerking from his ever-changing view but he couldn't feel it and from the sounds that must have been coming from him but sounded so far away. Darkness crept in from his peripheral. The volume in his ears was toning down. From panic stricken he entered into complete serenity. His last breath was drew at 12:22pm. He was 24 years old.

A Change In Attitude

HMP BelIs
Woodfields
Wd3 9WI
15th December 20—

Dear *mum,*

I hope your good. *Im sure* you heard what I got sentenced to. Its nothin. Ive done jail before and I'll do it again. Mama dint *raise* no fool hahaha. If *am* honest I cant take you cryin on da phone like dat. It *makes me* feel bad den im in a bad *mood* etc etc for the rest of the day.

AnYwaY ive booked a visit for you and Scarlett. *she says* she'll *come* for you at 9am *so* ~~you better~~ MAKE SURE YOUR READY!!

if any Of the lads *come* round tell *em* i *said* YO!'.

Do *me* a favour and *go* to Dale's and get *me* dat thing Off him. He *owes me* £50 too.

Ive been hearing you've been letting craig in the house again and *hes* up to his old

StUff. STOP! IT! I swear if I *see* him in here am gunna have him.

Im thinkin of getting Scarlett to StaY at yours to keep you company.

Right *im* Off *as* it *is* dinner time.

your favourite *son* =)
X

PS- *im* gunna need £100 at Ieast a month too.

HMP Bells
WoodfieldS
Wd3 9WI
19th January 20-

Hey babes,

I hope your ok? Im good. Back in da *gym.* Been doin press ups in da cell an feelin HENCH! scales say different though hahahaah. Oh I forgot to say that Danny H *is* here aswell as Duster and his cousin. We got it boxed *Off.* All we do *is* cook every night an buss bare joke.

I spoke to mY *mum* an she said she wants you to *go* back. She says she was getting a Iil out *Of* hand with the drink as it was ChriStmas an said *some* Stuff she shunt av.

I know itS not what you are *used* to but itS Cheaper for *me* to ring the house phone and I know you are *safe* as well as mY *mum.*

'Please *go* back!!!

Ive been told I need to do a behavioural course. I wasn't happy at firSt and I was kickin *Off* with OMU but I thought itS what ive been wanting to do for *ages.* see whatS broken an fix it. I thought it would help *us* to. I wud do anYthing for you. you know that don't Ya.

I love you *more* than life itS self. I don't know what I would do without you babY. I couldn't cope without you. I would do something Stupid I swear. Theres not too long to wait anYwaY. I'll be getting my Cat D in no time. So don't be goin anywhere yeah lool.

Im sorry for shouting on the phone da other daY too. I just get *so* angry n don't know what to do. I end up saYin things and we both know I don't mean it.
Danny H said that his sister saw you with Teri. I don't like or truSt her. Just keep that in mind.

Im gunna leave you a week and ill ring you either Monday or Tuesday.

Love you the most
Your man
XXX

H M P Gaterush
Coldford
Df3 910
20th June 20—

YOOOO!!!

Just got Ya *address Off* Scarlett! WatS dat gansta sayin? You Know man *is* up in da big cat B SYStem. Gotta Keep a G in real jail, Ya get meh hahaha.

No on a real itS cool here. Man get bare ~~sorsh~~ association and *ders* a better criminal class in a *sense.* ItS not too too bad *ere* as man respect each udda but when it pops bruv it pops *Off* differently. Man r cold ere.

To be honest I feel stitched up. Da judge fucKed me and dem pussYhole victims. Little grassin baStards. An dat brief just *seemed* to bend to the ~~prose~~ prosecution and da judge like *some* flaKe da wasteman.

Mi did tinK I wudda got life doe.

Tell *X* al *sort* him when I land Yeh? Tell him I ant forgot nutten an ive got him.

I heard bare DJs bin comin Woodfields and shuttin it down. I wish man was der. Id be getting all Kindsa gyal an ting an tiiiiing, Ya Zimmi dawg? *Eeee* haha.

Just a lil breathing space at the moment here Ya zeet. Am getting *some* good linKs wi man dat do *dis* reallY really. Big food comin our way.

Anyway av ad to get Scarlett in *wi mi* mum *so* she Keeps her eye on her haha. Cant av mans gyal movin slacK while im up in here. you Know I got dat mind control over DBO.

AnYWaY fam my boys hollerin me to do *some* PUll ups. yo I can do muscle ups now Yano. Im gonna be bolo when I land. MeK a man *seh* sutten haha.

Holla back yeh

D-Man

H M P Gaterush
Coldford
Df39IO
llth AuguSt 20-

Wow

I ~~cant~~ can not believe I ant got a card Off you.

Dat *was* a shock. Is dat a *sign* Of things to come? ltS almost a given dat mY friends are gunna disappear but I dint think you ~~wud~~ would.

I don't even know what to say *as* I ant received a replY from you *so* im just guna 1eave it ere.

All because I asked you for some money. you think your ~~**srtug**~~ struggling den what about me, in here, you know, jail. Ya selfish you.

H M'P Gaterush
Coldford
Df39I0
1'1-th August 20-

Aww bbz

I think im done with my mum. She dint even *get* me a card man. Wtf!! OnlY u an my uncle. ~~Acurat~~ actuallY nah I *gOt* one Off my dad today. 2 *weeks* late but Still.

That behavioural course im on has *got* me thinking about that Other jail I was tellin you da lads are always on about. some feelings *gOt* Stimulated from this *exercise we* did there and I cant shake em. I told the facilitator on a one 2 one an she *was* over the moon, babes *im* talking super ~~exit~~ excited. She asked me what im goin to do with them? What da fuck *does* dat mean? What am I going to do with my feelins?

15th august

Yo babes it *was* mad. I *was* writing to you through association when the *screw* suddenlY locked my door. I thought *dis is* early. I jumped up and *saw* through the gap Of the door dat da opposite cells *were* shut too. Next ting da lads *were* talkin through da window saYin dat *dis* Kid gOt stabbed up from top to bottom bY several guys and his leg was chopped ~~dwn~~ down to the bone. CraZY eh? ltS mad but itS entertaining at the same time ca we'Ve *gat* summet to talk about now. some excitement in our conversations ca *dis* Place *is* full Of lifers and long termers and it *is* depressin to fuck. Some ant bin out since the *90s* and even their *words* are *dressed* in FILA an ELLESSE an I Know it sounds mad but even when dey talk about summet simple I can *see* da 0ld ford Cortina. Av bin in a yearish and they say av Stil gOt the smell of road on me haha.

What am I going to do with these feelins? CraZY bitch eh lol.

Am glad you'Ve left my mums ca she int right anyway. Better you StaY at home. I wr0te to Terra an he ant hollad me *so* at the minute am saYin fUCk him.

Anyway babes ill av rung you before dis reaches Ya.

Love you
D *xxx*

HMP Gaterush
Coldford
Of3 910
11th September 20-

HeY juSt a quick script. ~~*My bOy*~~ This guy I know put da transfer to that therapy jail in for *me* and ive bin accepted. I should be der within the next week or *so.*

Im lookin forward to *see* what dis Place has to Offer. I tried to get this guy I Chill with in here to *come* but he says he int sittin wi bare man dat could possiblY be peedos and hittin a nerve and breakin down cryin. I get it but I dint at the *same* time as something could *come from dis.*

Oh Yeh, 3 man got stabbed on K wing this afternoon. someone got slashed in the neck on the waY back *from* education and *someone* got stabbed in the eye yesterday in education.

Love you
D xx

HMP Setters
Heggersbourne
HB12 7fH
23rd October 20-

Dear babes lol,

Being here over the laSt few weeKs has blown *my mind.* They have these *massive* argumentS in the big *room* where we all *sit* and when itS done they carry on *as* normal. No fightS or stabbings, nothin. But we'll go bacK in for another meeting and they basicallY carry on ~~form~~ *from* where they left off just *as ferocious as* before. Mad. They *sit* in there grassin each other up or tellin each other how much they love each other. *Im* lOSt but on the other hand I feel *as* though I *am* found. I *am* completely shoCKed at what happens in the *room* but at the *same time* I feel safe(ish) and Kinda appreciate how theY go about things. They *seem* to argue and get to a point. I thinK baCK to growing up and we never got to a point. Theres about

10 million argumentS Still open ready to be carried on *from* when I was 8 til now. TheY move on, well ~~moost~~ *moSt* do *some* cling on harder then *me.* They vote them off if they cant get with the 'process'. All in all *itS* OK. ltS just *summet am* not used to.

cant wait to *see* u.

Love D

PS- *im* guna get this parole

PPS- ill do all this craZiness for you

xx

HMP Setters
Heggersbourne
HB12 7TH
7th February 20-

Hey babs,

so I took a group today an itS like *deez* man all jus turned on *me.* It ~~woz~~ was mad. I was getting *pissed Off* with them all but at the *same* time I was still able to hear *dem* out which was craZY. NormallY I *go* into *myself,* heavy breathin to death and thinkin 'am guna hit *someone, am* guna hit *someone·*. But I recognised that pattern and for the first time I was able to 'function' as they say whilst *my* pulse was through the roOf. They call it managing. Wow. you almost feel powerful. I felt in control for the first time in that moment. It tapers off a Iil cuz I was left feelin as if theY'd done *me* a wrong all daY as normallY hittin them would leave *me* with something to brag about to *mY* pals and I would be congratulated and I would have a bigger rep which helps you out on da roads. ltS liKe currency. I would be richer in a sense.

Anyway *im* Still feelin, I don't know, jus n0t good. The bastards lol.

PoSt card StYle letters for you now *seems* though av got the phone in the cell brap brap haha

Love you always
D
xx
'PS - I thinK I was neglected as a Child. They were on *dis* kid about it and described it and shared their own experiences. They sounded just like mine. WTF!? :S

HMP Setters
Heggersbourne
HB12 7TH
17th JUIY 20-

Heeeyaaa,

Babes this Place *is* craZY. I realised 2 things. Ive slowed my thought *process* down
and learnt how to be kind to myself. The slowin of the thought *process* came from
one Of the lads havin a group and after he spoke Of juSt doin it,' they *said* no it was
a choice. I was feelin the anger comin up from this statement but I felt it and let it
pass and sat there and thought about it. I thought back to that night and realised I
was thinking Of mY boys and mY rep and I needed to be *as* far from the humiliation
as possible so did what I THOUGHT I had to, Ya get me? From that group I could
see that fr0m my initial *response* in *groups* and communitY *meetings* after I could
choose summet different. What? I dont know Yet but I am observing people go about

things a certain way but it reallY, (this *is* a new
word for me) fruStrates me when
theY don't do what Ya telling dem. *As* for the
kind to Yaself ting, theres this painting
on da *wing* that *says* ·a kinder you to you, *is* a
kinda you to others'. Now it *seemed*
to make *sense* on a *surface* level but dint make
sense to me at the same time *if* Ya
get meh. I mean I knew there was summet in it
but I dint know what. How do you
be kind to Yaself???? :S craZY talk init hahaha.
AnYWaY ~~lost~~ last night I was writing
some stuff down that was coming to me and I
was getting 'frustrated' (lol) when I
hit mYSelf *in* the forehead with mY palm like
Ya do when Ya think 'stupid stupid'.
That's when that paintin on da wall made *sense.*
I could *see* how that stuff impactS
on you to hit Yaself *so* you don't think no way
to do it to others. I could *see* that in
those momentS of frUStration that you feel to
attack (slowing the thought *process*
down, and breaking down situations) mans
movin savage with the therapiZZY looool.

18th JUIY

sorry babbi-boo boo I ad a cuppa an watched tellY last night. AnYWaY todaY there was a new guy to av a round robin for him (a round robin *is* where they introduce themselves and we go round one bY one saYin our name and WhY we are here, *sometimes* the ~~nerw~~ new guy *Chooses* to go last. AnYwaY I mostlY *say* im here for you, mY daughter and mY mum, and *deez* man dat av bin *ere* for time always *seem* to *snigger* and kinda like shake der head. WTf man. WhY else would I be here??? Some waste man *ere* Yano.

Anyway im *Off so* I'll write when I av summet else to whinge about haha

Love you more everYdaY here

Its strange
D
Xx

PS -They been talKin bout *needs* and wantS for *ages* and I hav bin lost. I only just got that what we need are what motivates *us* to behave how we do. If we unconsciouslY perceive dat our *needs* have been detached we act in a way to get them bacK. one guy in the group who's bin ere for *ages* started on about his. He *said* that he *needs* respect *so* in the moment his victim 'disrepected' him he acted violentlY to get it baCK. I related inStantlY. Babes I need *some* stuff ~~sned~~ sendin in on Abraham Maslow and the Hierarchy *of Needs.*

HM'P Setters
Heggersbourne
HB12 7TH
3rd January 20-

HeYa,

I wasn't looking forward to having Christmas Off but it was nice to kick back an ~~waeth~~ watch tellY and not drowned in emotion whether itS mine or *someone* elses.

AnYwaY I dint fUllY switch Off as I was still reflecting and havin some big conversations with people that are signed Off (finished and ready to move on) and I learnt some more stuff. I was enquiring about control an all he said was a few words and I thought wow. I had to jump *on* da phone an ring mY mum. He basicallY spoke about how we look for control in our lives and don't like it when we feel out Of control. He *said* he'd *seen* me *in* the big room *in* community meetings an saw how red I *go* when I say something and it either *gets dismissed* or the person does the opposite. He said he saw that I meant well but people don't have to take what I say onboard every time. He asked me how I felt in those ~~momnetS~~ momentS. I searched my feelings and found it but didn't know the name. He passed me a book bY *someone* called Brene Brown, its called Daring GreatlY ... or summet. I read it a couple pages and it has research *in* it and all dat but *one* page stuck out. It asked loads of people how they felt when vulnerable, there was like 20 bullet pointS and I dint connect with any until I saw 'when I want to punch *someone* before theY punch me'.

Babes. I had to sit down. I thought ehh, I always thought I was angry when I was in conflict and that happened. I could not believe that I felt vulnerable all those times, too many times to recall babes. It all fell into Place. In those momentS *is* when the glass floor fell through and I thought I was out *of* control. I fought hell for leather to get that control back. Whaat!? CraZY babes. I am learning *some* need to know shit but I feel like nobody knows this Stuff. I jumped *on* the phone and

apoIogised profusely to mY mum for all the times I had reacted and been a
nightmare. All the vulnerabIe feelings came flooding back from Childhood and I
realised why I went down the road I did to get complete control in Beshill babes.
That's whY everyone moves like dat in Beshill and da rest Of da rough areas *in* da
world. Mind. Blown. Boooom!! All those times ive blown up for fUCk all. ltS
embarrassing now. I *see* that I do have a choice more. I *see* whY them guys in the
community meetings and groups annoyed and frustrated me to death. I feel reallY
free.

AnYwaY mans *gone* yeah

Skrr
Skrr
=)
LUV Ya babbeh!
D xx

PS again lol - I need a book called counselling for Toads. Av bin told it will help *me* along bY one of the lads that are signed off. It turns out that this anger I *used* to feel all the time *is* actuallY a secondary emotion. They say that when someone feels sad or hurt they learn to convert it into anger. This way they don't feel the perceived 'pain' of the primary emotions as they carry heavy baggage and associations from the paSt or what they call unresolved *issues.* **Am** I rollin or what ere babes. This stuff *is* powerful. I’m lookin back now and *mY* 0ld life *is* Startin to become fUZZY but *my* past isn't, if that makes ~~SeS~~ sense to Ya. MY future *is* Startin to look Clear. □

HMP Setters
Heggersbourne
HB12 7TH
10th februarY 20-

yes bro,

Thanks for the letter. Yeh am gud. JuSt getting on with it. How are you? Hows the
new jail treating you? I know dem man in der will be full Of stuff and dont even
know it. Your *missed* here tho. The group dunt feel the same. But that's loss and
grief init, no matter how large or small we gotta get through the *process.*

Arrggh Steve's still being Stubborn as fuck. He still wont admit that he set out to
do it. And he flew Off the handle with Brian when he asked him if he thinks his son
has forgiven him. Bare drama and palava. Jack's getting thru it though. He's gunna
be the next risin star in there. He sitS there hardlY ~~socali~~ socialisin on da wing an
dat *so* I invited him to come plaY COD BOPS with *us* an he won the first game!!

TUh blouse an skirt! I had to tun up for him an change mY load out. I said if he wins again we're gunna bar him *cant wtch face* lol.

Did you get a reply off your sister? That's sum heaVY stuff there pal but you'll get through and be a better man for it. you are one of the most dedicated people ive ever met. Its been a privilege our kid haha.

Yeh make sure you keep on with the Studies. Ive got a few things in the pipeline with the support worker Stuff *so* im going down the counselling route once I get these replies back *so* I know which pathway to take.

Gotta stay flexible an have a few options in *case* things *go* pear shaped.

Right im off cuz itS Ali's birthday and we havin a meal and cake for it. Benny *says* ‘yo’ man Of few *words* that he *is*. Callum *says* he can do more burpees than you an AndY says he wrote to you firSt but you Chose to reply to me firSt. I told him it will be in the post man lol.

Keep on keeping on my brother. your journey *is* nearlY up.

DarrYI

HMP Setters
Heggersbourne
HB12 7TH
20th March 20-

HeY Linda,

Yeah im good. I hope you are too. Yeah I thought I would try this prison companion thing as I am trYing new things and wanted to stretch myself if you know what I mean.

I *am* on a Therapeutic community and we are encouraged to challenge ourselves *so* this is difficult for *me* and a little anxietY inducing.

I have been trying to write something for a writing competition but I *am* Struggling with my creativity.

I haven't listened to any Of that but I will tune into Radio 6 and give my reviews haha.

Thank you for the support on my music thing. I trUIY appreciate the acknowledgement and support.

Im going to leave it here for now but I hope to hear *from* you soon.

yours sincerely

DarrYI Cobbs

HMP Setters
Heggersbourne
HB12 7TH
11th June 20-

Yoooo,

JuSt had *mY* board and I gOt signed off. I feel full Of confidence. ItS amaZing how you feel when people give you praise and recognition for your triumphs and positiveIy give you feedbaCK on how to better yourself and worK on weaKnesses. Well you have to be open to feedbaCK as it *is* easy to just bat it off and StaY all fUCKed up in your bubble. I *am* patching up *so* many holes in *my* bUCKet its unreal babes. I recentlY *saw* what they meant when I Kept saying that I *was* here for you, *my mum* and daughter. Its because if you were all, heaven forbid, to pass away or Ieave *me,* that I would fall to pieces and revert baCK to OId, destructive ways *as* I did it 'for you lot'. When I actuallY do it for *me so* that Whether anyone *is* in *my* life

or n0t I can Still maintain what I have built and continue on the *same* course. Babes
during that board I realised that I have done *more* than ive probablY done in the
last *10* years out there. I have run multiple poetry and yoga Classes. I have wr0te,
devised, set up an recruited people to taKe part in eventS. I have tooK part in *some*
Of the most embarrassing tasKs in *my* life and n0t let the feelings hold *me* baCK (n0t
everyone tooK part as their feelings held them back). I have helped countless people
on their journey and *more* importantlY I have learnt to trust, be open and share
What I *go* through. I *am* ShOCKed at hOW I have behaved preViOUSlY due to *my* own upbringing and how I put that on Others. This Place has given *me my* life bacK and I
am in control. I have *made* conscious good decision after good decision and it has
brought the best out of *me* and Others. All the times I tooK *myself* out of *mY*
comfort zone and challenged *myself* has given a *new* perspective, no, a true
perspective Of what I can do and where *my* abilities lie. LooKin at how *me* and *mY*
peers behaved caused *me* to *see* how I fit in a roIe when I *am* around them. I

haven't been able to be *myself. I'm* n0t putting it on them as I *am* now taKin myself
away an able to build new, positive peers who share *mY new* outlOOK I cant wait to
start going to crossfit Classes, yoga, salsa dancing with you and taKing part in
ParKruns for fun and charity. I cant wait for us to build our little empire and *go*
into property once *we* have our feet firmlY under the table in our own jobs. I
couldn't thinK Of anYthing better than to worK with you, *my* heart and soul. This
Place allowed *me* to trUIY appreciate people and especiallY you. MY entitlementS
have been dropped and I Know that you do for *me* out of unconditional Iove and I
Ioved you *more* and *more* whilst being here. It dawned on *me more* and *more* how I
am in the right relationship with the right *woman.* I couldn't have done this with
anyone. You have let *me* reSt assured that you are *mine* and that propelled *me*
further as a lot Of Others on here are in destructive unstable relationships that holds them back. Understanding Maslow's Hierarchy Of *Needs* and the Hierarchy of competence along with Bloom's Taxonomy has opened my mind up metaPhYSiCallY

beyond the confines Of my cranium. I know I rant and *use* mad metaphors but there's no Other way for *me* to convey my *message.* That leads *me* to being underStood and FEELIN understood bY those around *me.* Being able to communicate effectiVelY what I think and feel in such a way that those around *me* utterlY and t0tallY get *me.* This was a deep-seated thing for *me* as I always felt neglected and bY the way *side* due to people n0t understanding *me* or believing *me.* Learnin Of group dynamics and how there can be power Struggles. seein who likes what *see* within a dYnamic and seein what seat I like. Challenging my beliefs was a *game* changer too as that allowed *me* to *see* the error Of my ways. How those beliefs leave you stuck in a mould or type cast forever. Here, through lookin at my familY, friends, partners, area, even the media and *music* etc I *see* how I was influenced. I *see* how I was fuelled bY unresolved *issues* that caused *me* to *seek* my outlet through the StreetS on to Others. Being here an encouraged to be who I want to be has brought about my creative *side* again which in turn has allowed *me* to devise ways around life and how to manoeuvre out Of situations. MY creatiVitY *is* my healthY outlet as well as fitness. I have related to people in such a deep and broad level that I cann0t believe it as I dont know mY own familY and friends on such a level. I can now feel the warmth of support *from* those around *me* and can accept and action their advice. I have devised a Plan Of action *from* now and on release that *is* realistic to keep *me* away *from* badness and safe. *If* anYthing out Of the blue *does* pop up I can change my Plans accordingly and work with what I have. And as for us. I have never trusted, loved and appreciated someone as much as you. our conversations have been ones of tru depth and warmth. you are the onlY person I know outside Of here properly. We have bared our souls and been sheltered bY the Other. We have had our disagreementS about things but that *is* because we have had our own ideas from such a young age and 'expectations' makes us think that that is the accepted and that is what will happen. We have finallY converged and trUlY have Plans that are 'ours'. N0t mine and n0t yours. I can never say that I have had Plans

with anyone. I have always had the 'ejector seat' option open at all times. Scarlett,
you are everything to *me.* you mean the world to *me* and I am glad and honoured to
call you my partner. This Place and sentence and decision to *come* has allowed us to
be an absolute titan of a couple. I can n0t wait to *see* you on Saturday.

Love you (as you know)

D
xxxx

The Caterers

Walking out of work on a very hot summers day, Amy was glad to have finished. It had been a long few weeks in the office and the project had finally come to a close. Her boss had been a complete arsehole with her and this had got her thinking of either a transfer to another office or a completely new job. These thoughts were on the back burner as it was Friday, and she was ready to party with her girls. She had set up a group chat in the final meeting earlier that day to get the ladies fired up for a night of drinking, dancing and fun. All the girls had agreed which was fantastic and they all decided to meet at Deana's at 8pm for pre-drinks and pre-selfies. Amy was a catch. Educated, career driven and got the personality as well as the looks with and air of confidence and class. A 28-year-old stunner who believed she helped as much as she could.
She was a mean girl growing up but during her time at university she moved away from that crowd. She smiled to herself as she made her way to her car. Amy was extremely excited as she hadn't been out for months and needed to let her hair down as the feelings of work were really getting on top of her. Reaching her car, Amy sat in the drivers' seat and updated her socials before setting off. She was hoping that Ben, a guy she liked and had kissed in the past, would pick up on it and make an appearance tonight. Push start, reverse gear and Amy was heading home. She enjoyed her drive home as it gave her time to decompress. She had

become quite adept at lessening her feelings from work during her drive home so it didn't affect her too much at home. Coming to the top of a blind hill, Amy did not have any time or opportunity to move out of the way of the car that had just emerged over the brow of the hill on her side of the road. The bumpers made contact and crumpled. Compressing into the engine block. The engine was pushed on to the cars frame which, in turn, snapped Amy's tibia and fibia, pushing the lower halves under her seat. The steering wheel and dashboard came down on her femurs breaking them clean, causing the half still attached to her pelvis to rip through the skin allowing the medullary cavity to be looked down. The sudden force of the cars' collision and the rapid rate of deceleration threw Amy forward where she smashed her sternum and fractured all twelve pairs of ribs on the airbag, causing massive internal damage. When the cars hit, they swung round. Amy's car went through the farmers fence, down the slight banking and finished on its side. Glass and debris from the chassis and under carriage littered the ground around the vehicle. Amy's life expired instantly as she sustained massive trauma to her frontal lobe and her aorta snapped from making contact with the airbag. But yet, she felt present in her body but she was outside her car. She was disorientated in the sense that wasn't her normal self, but it was a disorientation that she hadn't felt before. She could hear some heavy feet coming towards her but she couldn't move. Then she was grabbed from behind and thrown. This experience was also, different. When she landed, she was in a cemetery at night on, what felt like, her hands and knees. This time she could move, but only within a short range as if encased in a glass box in an exact outline of her on her hands and knees with a gap 1 inch either way. The footsteps trudged up alongside her she couldn't turn to look as if fear had gripped her. A huge hand which felt powerful and broad, way broader than anything human, with unnaturally large fingers grabbed her by the back of the head and lifted her off the ground. 'Look!' the figure said. In front of Amy was a grave. She started to feel heat. Real heat, like when your too close to a bonfire. The grave was freshly filled with the dirt still a mound and a wooden cross at the head. The dirt began to come alive and filter away from the grave like it was being forced up out of it. It was moving fluidly, almost like liquid. It continued until it exposed a fire. A coffin could just about be made out, but it wasn't burning. The heat was unbearable for Amy who was panicking as she did not understand what was going on. The figure pulled her away from the fire a few feet and then launched her into the flames. Amy screamed with enough vivacity to shatter every glass in the world. Intense heat. Pain. Burning. Darkness. 'Open' was said and Amy's eyes opened wider than they had ever been open before. She was in a darkroom, but it wasn't a room, it felt large and vast. It echoed. it was pitch black but she could see herself when she looked down even though there was no visible light source. She was crying and shivering as she could not understand what was happening. She could remember it being a nice hot day where she was making plans with her friends about going out and now she was in a dark room that had an incredibly strong stench and was terribly cold. She was muttering to herself in her confused state when for the third time she heard that voice. 'Silence'. When the voice spoke, she did what was commanded but not on her own volition. It was just happening. Her body just made her look at the grave, it made her open her eyes and now it made her silent. Heavy footsteps began making their way towards her but she couldn't see anyone. They sounded close enough for her to see someone if they were there but far enough that they would take a little while to be physically near her. She remained quiet but tried to move. She felt like she was shackled by heavy chains with diamond shaped metal spikes that were around her wrists and ankles pulling her taut but there was nothing she could see. She could see both her wrists free from anything but the feeling was to the contrary. Suddenly there was a screech right above her head. It was so piercing that she had to close her eyes tight. She looked up and saw a huge head the length and width of a saloon car. It was as white as bone with protruding sharp edges and corners. It was hard for Amy to make out what exactly it was as she could have sworn that it was changing shape. It had no eyes just deep black holes the size of bin lids that blended into the surroundings. There was no mouth. Its forehead was wavy on the edges for some reason and it tapered down to a point at the chin. It was almost like a masquerade mask or some sort of skinned cattle skull that she had never seen before. The stench was horrific and putrid. The closest thing in Amy's memory is of the abattoir she used to drive past as a child with the family to the seaside. The head began to get smaller. Amy realised the head had a body, and it was standing to its full height. The footsteps started again but they were much smaller sounding than the huge figure that she knew was there. The footsteps continued to get closer and the figure was shrinking with every step. The figure stopped about 50 feet away from her. It was in long raggedy, thick black robes that moved in such a way it appeared they were alive. It was as if the material was tar or crude oil. The figure must have been 12-15 feet tall. Broad shouldered, unusually long arms and hands that looked, from the distance Amy was at, to be bone white with extremely long talon like fingers. Amy felt the atmosphere change. She believed the figure was getting angry. Its head, she realised was hooded and it looked as if the expression on it was changing. Its chest was heaving. It hunched as if ready to fight. The temperature dropped even further, and Amy knew way before the new temperature she should've been able to see her breath. The figure cast its huge taloned claw back and with a lightning switch of the shoulders throw it forward as if it had just thrown a fast ball and Amy felt the deepest, sharpest pain ever in her solar plexus. She saw its claw was empty yet it still felt like it had just launched a searing hot spear into her chest. She knew nothing had come out the other side but it felt it had gone a mile deep within her. Into a region of herself that she had not known existed. The absolutely agonising pain tearing into her was still travelling deep and fast and then all of a sudden, she was breathless and sad. Something had been hit inside her and she knew exactly what it was. Now she felt dead. When the figures spear struck it felt as if her energy had been sucked from her. It felt as if her biomechanical switches had all been flicked off. The figure had speared her soul. It brought both hands forward in front of him with the palms facing Amy, fingers outstretched and that's when she felt the spear coming back the way it came but at a much slower pace. This time the spear felt heavy and the pain which was a 100 on the scale compared to anything she had felt before, now felt like a 10. This pain was the new 100. It was like a constant onslaught on her nervous system. It was as if needles were coming out of every pore in her skin and It felt as if she was receiving very high voltage electric shocks every nano second. Amy's body was throwing itself around violently in her invisible shackles.

The feeling was as if she was being dragged across a field, but every blade of grass was a razor blade. The pain was an emanating one that started in a vast unknown within herself that came through her bones, blood, organs and skin. It came in waves and droves. Nothing that a human body in the realm of the living could ever experience. Amy screamed. This scream dwarfed the one by the grave. This scream traverses space and time and will be felt as a natural disaster on earth. This scream is the sustenance of the Caterers. This scream is beyond guttural. This scream is the sound of the soul trying to cling on as it is dragged from the host ready for consumption. All the while several memories tore through her mind of her taunting Kate at school. Amy wondered if this is why this was happening to her.

*****

Dum! dum! dum! dum! dum! Chris rapped heavily on the door. He was feeling extremely unwell. His nose was running down his philtrum, over his lip and into his mouth. This did not faze Chris in the slightest. He had one thing at the top of his list of things to do and his mind was set on it. He was getting impatient and began to bang on the door again. There was more venom in it this time and he could now hear someone moving around inside. Something large and heavy was being pulled away from the door. Large bolts were drawn back. The door didn't open immediately as it sticks due to it being slightly larger than the frame due to it being new from the recent police raid. Chris shoulder barged it feebly as he is a slender man, ravaged by the effects of Class A drugs. The door finally opened as the man on the inside prised it open by placing his foot on the wall. He motioned for Chris to get inside. The man wasn't happy to see Chris and could have easily become violent against him but refrained as he knew Chris would give him some of what he had. Chris squeezed past and made his way up the stairs that were immediately across from the door. He took them two at a time, turned the corner, made his way a short way down the landing to another set of stairs and climbed those two at a time. He was in a big rush as he was feeling really bad. He was sweating profusely but cold. He reached the door to the sole room at the top of the stairs. His heart was beating hard before and it increased further still, but not through physical exertion, through the anticipation of the treat he has in store for himself. He makes his way past the others who are sat on the floor, up against the walls and sprawled on the bed. He makes his way to the corner of the room, his corner. His own little personal 1.2m2 of land. It is next to a bedside cabinet where he can place his 'make happy' kit. He takes off his bag, gets out his rubber tubing, lemon, knife to cut it, spoon, lighter and cotton bud. He reaches into his mouth and retrieves the bag of heroin from a gap between a molar and his wisdom tooth. Fast forward and the plunger has been pushed all the way down and the heroin has been flushed down into his vein and is making its way up the arm, hurtling towards the heart. His hand falls away from the needle which is still in his arm, and he drops back against the wall with a light thud. He can taste it at the back of his throat, and he is excited as he now knows it will be strong. The heroin enters Chris' heart via the superior vena cava where it enters the right atrium with the rest of the deoxygenated blood, it is sucked down into the right ventricle through the tricuspid valve and fires up the pulmonary artery to his lungs. There, the blood the heroin is being transported with, becomes oxygenated, makes it way back to the heart via the pulmonary vein and into the left atrium. Here it gets pulled down into the left ventricle and goes through the aorta and finds its way to every organ and area of Chris' body. As the heroin rushes to the brain the opioids in it bind with receptors and releases a flood of dopamine. Chris sinks into a euphoria. He feels the warm flushing of the skin, a dry mouth and his arms are even heavier. His stress disappears, his traumas and anxieties dissipate. All his senses and perceptions begin to slow down, including his nervous system and brain. His breathing is getting shallow. He slips down the wall to the floor so now his head is resting on his chest. The collar of his jacket trapped between his chin and chest. His breathing has been restricted further. The heroin is too strong for Chris and his body tries to reject it. He starts to vomit but the passageway is severely restricted. He is in too much of a stupor to attempt to move. He can't breathe. His body violently rocks for several moments. Chris is slowly slipping. His eyes are glassy and slightly open. He sees two long, white, spindly and bony hands rise up and overlap over his torso and rapidly lower on to him. He feels the sensation of being forced down like there was a bar with several hundred kilograms on it that had been dropped on him. He stumbles through a second door unable to understand anything. He was shackled by spiked chains he couldn't see which pulled him tight in every direction. Chris was glad to be away from the skeleton face as there was a deep intensely emanating emotional pain of fear, vulnerability, shame and disappointment multiplied many fold beyond what he felt on earth, alive. He believed he was dead but still felt pain and was panting hard. How can i breathe he thought as he was on his hands and knees. Getting some form of bearings, he looked around to find he was in some kind of cave. A charcoal black cave with red hues. It wasn't made of rock, but of something that resembled ember. It was smooth clean. There was a rotten methane smell that felt as thick as smog that filled the space. There was more light in this place emanating through the red areas than in the previous arena where he lost his soul. He turned round and saw that there was no door and the 'room' had become vast like the last one. He felt a presence at his 2 o'clock so he spun round from his 6 and 7 o'clock to face what he felt. Stood, or rather hovering, was another 12 foot 'being '. It wasn't robed. It was naked except for raggedy, dirty white loin cloth. It had extremely broad shoulders, a barrel chest with ribs prominent. It had a thin waist and abnormally long upper and lower limbs. It had what looked like rotted, brown, purple and green skin pulled tight over its large muscles and bones, looking sinewy. Its face resembled Anubis from Egyptian mythology with its pointy ears except with massive degradation and decay. There was a straggly lion's mane at the back of its head and two large shiny, like onyx, black canine teeth. It was not stood proud; it was stood slightly slouched with its head almost resting on its chest. Even with such a lack of pride in its stance it was still oozing danger and physically intimidated Chris. Things moved under its skin that could only be presumed to be insects from how they moved. Different insects of different sizes and capabilities. The being slowly raised its right arm in front of it and stopped just above head level. It had a crook in its arm and fingers in a puppet master position. Chris was raising up off the ground at the same pace as the being's hand. He stopped about 2 foot off the ground. The being lowered his hand but Chris remained. Chris still felt the pain of the soul removal as the being glided across the floor towards him. It stopped within Its own personal space and glared at Chris. Chris' eyes burnt from the penetrating stare of the being. It had no eyeballs. Just deep black sockets. A flame could be seen in a great distance in its sockets. It stood to its full height and at this Chris was somehow forced to push his chest out. It felt as if an invisible hand had reached into his chest cavity, grabbed his spine and was pulling forward. This thought brought back the memory of how the door to the house he died in had to be opened. The being slowly moved its hand towards Chris' hand with its index finger and thumb at the ready to pluck something. When it made contact with his skin there was a slight red flash as it grabbed something just below skin level. As soon as it touched it Chris went blind with pain and threw his body violently, or as violently as he could in his floating subdued position. The being was pulling something from Chris' naked body. He was struggling to make out what this was as he was in so much pain. The being was pulling a thread that was zipping up and down Chris' body and causing his nervous system taxing pain. It was as agonising as the first ordeal, but this was

different. The previous one kept him wide awake but
this one was knocking him out. He didn't have time to register the pain before he was out. His heart was firing at a maximum he had never experienced in the earthly realm. He began to realise that the 'thing' was unravelling his nerves like a piece of cotton. It was slavering large globules of blackish green saliva from the corners of its mouth. Some of it made its way to the front and ran the length of the canines. It was getting excited. It kept pulling its hand towards itself as the nerves were ripping through the skin like wire through dry wall. Chunks of meaty flesh and gristle speckled off the nerves. It was taking Chris' breath away. He was saying in breathless tones "No more, please, no more". When it got stuck behind a bone, ligament, muscle or tendon, it just yanked it out of the spinal cord. It snatched out the brachial plexus, musculocutaneous, radial, median and ulna nerves from the arm. It moved on to the nerves in the torso, pulling them out through the skin of the stomach. The skin bursting and splashing blood on to Chris, the floor and the Anubis headed being with every tug. By the time it was finished, there was a spool of nerves on the floor and Chris' body was in a total mess. His skin, from the tip of his toes all the way to his face, was ripped to shreds. Due to the deep lacerations you would have been forgiven for thinking that razor wire had been wrenched across him every

which way. Bone and muscle were exposed, through the gaping long furrows of open wounds as well as remnants hanging out. Even though it was over the pain was still there accompanied by the separate pain of the soul removal. He could not understand how he still 'felt' even though his nerves had been ripped from his body. The being seemed to become angry from its behaviour as it became tense and squeezed its arms together in front of its chest with clenched fists. It forcefully flung back its arms, bending forward at the hips and roared powerfully. The power was such that it blew Chris into oblivion.

*****

Alesha closed the door behind her. She had just dropped off several bags of clothes and electricals to local charities. She felt a band-aid of happiness over her overarching emotional wounds. Throwing her keys on the kitchen counter, she opened the fridge and got out the sole item, a bottle of white wine. She grabbed two wine glasses and walked into the living room to have one last look. It was empty and it was slightly upsetting. This had been a happy home and was furnished very well. Thoughts of some of the good times flashed on her memory screen as she moved on and up the stairs. Alesha walked into the bathroom where she had left some items for later use and ran her bath. She sat on the floor, leaning over the side of the bath swirling her hand on the surface of the water in a dream world, silently sobbing. She had not been able to recover from the heartbreak of her partner leaving. He had been seeing someone else for a while and decided to tell Alesha on their fourth anniversary, several weeks ago. It had been a very rocky and tumultuous time for her. It had been sudden for her, and she was in shock. She wanted to go round to the 'other' woman's house and smash her head in. She sat outside Emma's house and just watched, for hours on end. She would follow Andrew or Emma to work or shopping. She was all torn up inside and could not eat. She had lost weight and her confidence was through the floor. She had never imagined her life without Andrew and did not know what to do with herself or life now that there was this void. She had distanced herself from her friends and took many days off work as everything was just too unbearable. Alesha's friends meant well but they seemed to want her to forget too quickly the best times of her life and she didn't want to hear a bad word about Andrew. A very obvious best-known secret was that Alesha kept all this alive and defended him as she wanted him back. Conversations always lead to Andrew and she just felt that the world was against her and her relationship. It was a situation that weighed heavy on her. The bath was halfway full and she started to fill her two glasses with the wine and resumed to swirl the water but this time from the side of the bath. The bathroom was filling with steam as the bath was so hot. Bath full, she undressed and very tentatively got in. Steam danced, swirled and licked off the top of the water. Quickly acclimatising she sunk in and the water rose to within an inch from the top of the tub. She reached for her phone and began to compose a lengthy email that she was going to send to a colleague's work address, she knew that it would not be seen until a few minutes after 9 am. The email comprised of several short emails intended for various family and friends. She removed the lock on her phone so it could be easily accessed as there were some videos to provide some form of closure for her loved ones. She had been drinking throughout and had finished both glasses of wine. Placing her phone in a towel on the floor she settled back in and reached for the cutthroat razor blade. She locked it into place with a click and ever so gently and swiftly slashed open her left wrist. It was surprisingly painless and gave her the confidence to go further. Blood oozing out of her wound, changing the colour of the bath water. She let her hand slip into the water and watched it for a second and thought it mixed as it does when one places a paint covered brush into a glass of water to clean it. The water and paint exist as two separate entities for a while, the paint twisting and turning in the water, sometimes hitting a surface and bouncing off, until it eventually envelopes the water. Moving her mind on to stage two, in one move she inhales deeply, closes her eyes, tilts her head back, exposing her neck and swiftly catches it. The blow was relatively light but the proficiency from the blades engineering leaves her left jugular gaping and spurting blood the height, length and breadth of the bathroom. Alesha's eyes bulge through fear of the amount of blood. She is terrified. She is writhing around in the tub causing blood coloured water to flow over the side. The blood, pumped from her left ventricle, round the aorta, down the arteries, into the capillaries and exiting through the severed venules and veins and never making it back into the heart through the vena cava. The heat of the water has expanding all -her capillaries and allowing for more blood to move around her efficiently. The pulsating and intermittent rhythm of blood from the jugular was of great volume and this was the strike that sapped the most of Alesha's strength. She slipped under the water, writhing minimally now. The last thought to pass through her mind was that Andrew would be happy. Her life expired at 8:13 pm. Blasted from the volcano looking cave of the Anubis being. Alesha landed with a skull crushing thud. The equilibrium re-calibrated and she was actually on the floor rather than up against a wall as originally felt. This space was ambiently lit from an unknown source and appeared to be a narrow pit, reminiscent of a crudely dug well without the brickwork. It was more like rock this time but that of cooled volcanic ash, very rough and course. Alesha was still under massive duress from the soul removal and the nerve tearing. Weary and on shaky legs she stood up. The walls moved back several feet with a low vibrational rumble. There was a slight musty smell in the air that was vaguely noticeable compared to the other two realms. She took two painful and slow steps forward and the walls moved back between twenty and thirty foot this time. She was feeling defeated and did something that resembled crying due to her shredded facial skin and lack of living. The emotional hopelessness was magnified beyond anything she experienced on earth. She took several more awkward steps forward and the walls moved a mile back with a loud rumble that shook the ground and made Alesha fall to her knees. All of a sudden she began trembling and retching. A thick black bile falling out of her mouth. The smell was of manure and human faeces mix. The same stuff oozed out of the what was left of the pores in her hands, her tear ducts and eye secretion ducts, it flowed out of her ears and nose and began to coalesce into one huge mound. Copious amounts fell out of her. She felt as if she was dying again as she could not breathe, and the black bile seemed endless. With a deep inhalation, her eyes burst open. Her nostrils were assaulted with the searing smell of fresh manure and human faeces. She sat up and saw there was a hideous figure stood in front of her. The being stood smaller than the others at about 9ft and had a subtle feminine figure. The putrid smell was coming from it. "I am your bad deeds" it said in an electronic female voice.

"Wha, what!?" Alesha was confused. Nothing had been explained and nothing made sense. She turned around as she could hear footsteps advancing on her. There was a little girl angelic in appearance, with a smiling face that looked as if butter wouldn't melt walking towards her. In her hand she had some extremely shiny curved scissors as a tailor would have. Alesha felt a little safer at such a sight but then dropped lower into her pain and anguish as the little angel began to transform into a sickly child, whose skin had a yellowish tinge. The plumpness of her youth vanished and there stood a terrifying old lady with blackened teeth smiling at her. She let out a cackle which froze Alesha to the spot. At the same time, she grew to the same height as Alesha, grabbed her left arm and sliced up it as if she was slicing a jacket sleeve off her. She tugged it off from the elbow and then proceeded to slice up towards her neck, sometimes using the cutting action of the scissors whilst at other times the lower blade sliced her open with ease Alesha felt every slice. It was a third type of pain she felt in this arena. She could not get her head around how she was experiencing different kinds of pain as on earth it is more on severity then individualised and compartmentalised. This attack was twofold as it was the original cutting and then the witch would grab and tug, pull and rip large swathes of skin off her. It was pulled from the muscle that had a very sticky grip on the skin. The witch moved skilfully across and around the body. After the ordeal of skin removal, the witch unwound a nut that held the scissors together and, using the bigger and sharper half, stabbed Alesha underneath and between her legs. She penetrated her skin far back, braced one hand on Alesha's hip and began to saw her from back to front, blood falling out of her and splashing heavily beneath her. She stopped at the pubis, dropped the blade, reached inside the newly butchered chasm and began to route around inside her, yanking out organs. Alesha was now experiencing a fourth type of pain. Her chest heaving fast yet unevenly. Her mind screen was just of a bright white emptiness. She could not think, could not move and could not stop this monster pulling out her rectum, large and small intestine, stomach, liver, heart, lungs and the rest. Her head was being yanked around as the witch was pulling on her oesophagus. It eventually come loose and ripped her tongue, tonsils and the roof of her mouth out with it. When the tension of the oesophagus ended, Alesha's head lurched forward and rested on her chest. She had had just about all she could take. She opened her eyes to see the angelic face of the little girl who giggled turned and skipped off into the distance. As the girl disappeared, so did her power over Alesha as she fell to the floor into her strips of skin and organs. The hideous thing flipped Alesha over, forced its hand into her back, grabbed her spine in its fist and carried her off like a suitcase.

******

It was the hour the sun casts a golden light onto everything, and Ed was happy. He was on his way back from the shop with the requests of both his wife and kids. He appreciated the little things. He lived a mediocre life and did not mind one bit. He worked hard so his wife, Jo, didn't have to and so that he could provide for his children Stacy and Jeremy. They went on 2 holidays a year and just about kept up to date with electricals. Ed didn't care for material things so that worked almost as a saving that went towards his family. They were having steak to night which was his favourite and he couldn't wait to tuck in. The kids had requested some ice cream for after so the deal was for them to finish their vegetables and they could have a healthy scoop of ice cream. He had a surprise for them all after dinner too. He had booked a trip to Cuba. There would be swimming with the dolphins, jet skis and a helicopter ride for them all and a spa treatment for Jo who had recently recovered from Covid-19. He has them all believing that they weren't going anywhere this year but he had squirreled away some money from his plant selling business he had come up with to boost up his furlough money and keep him busy through the lockdown. He couldn't wait to see the kids' faces when all was revealed. This thought lit up Ed's face. This feeling was fleeting as a silver, blacked out Range Rover came screeching to a halt at the side of Ed. He had known this was coming for the last 12 years. He spun on a six pence and bolted. The occupants of the vehicle spilled out on to the pavement and road and began their pursuit. Ed risked life and limb as he darted across busy roads without looking. He would sooner get hit by a car then caught by his chasers. Over shopping parades and through parks, Ed wasn't losing them. He finally took a turn which was a mistake. He was cornered at the back of a row of shops. The wall was too high to climb, and he didn't have strength after such a lengthy run. He turned to the entrance of the alley but he was blocked in. They produced long, nasty looking knives and swords from up their sleeves and down the side of their joggers' legs. Zombie killer, rambo style bayonet and a mini samurai sword were out in all their glory. It was intimidating as they were all dressed in black jogging suits with gloves and full face, mouthless balaclavas with goggles over the eyes. Ed thought 'I am not dying today! '. He decided he was going to fight his way out. 'Come on then ya bastards!' and he ran at them. They did not flinch in the slightest and began to slash and stab at him. The first blow changed the tide and took all the steam out of Ed's game plan. The largest one lunged forward, plunging his zombie killer blade between the ribs, puncturing his intercostal muscles, lacerating the aorta and slicing through his right lung. Ed was done for. Adrenaline keeping him on his feet, he tried to cover up in a defensive boxer stance. A chop with the bayonet severed the right tricep, going through the epimysium, perimysium, endomysium and reverberating on impact with the humorous. The bicep kept the arm in its defensive position as the sliding filament theory of actin and myosin grabbing each other in the sarcomere of the tricep could not happen. Attempting anything with that muscle would leave him defenceless on his right side. The bayonet and zombie killer stepped back so the samurai could hack and chop at his leg. The first swing caught the illiotibial band on the side and kept on until it come out the quadricep. The back swing just whipped through the quad like a hot knife through butter and separated. Ed dropped to the ground. All three now swung top down as if wielding rounders bats. They leveraged on the balls of their feet, bouncing, full of adrenaline, and balanced with an outstretched empty hand until they crashed down with their weapons. Blood was pooling around Ed and covered the attackers and walls with spray. Ed now lay defenceless, but the attack carried on. Through the attack, another figure dressed in black and much larger, passed between two of them and in the blink of an eye extended to full height holding a weapon with both hands and brought the long wooden pole down hard which had a scythe on the end. Darkness. Ed was dumped on the floor by his bad deeds. He had been carried for some time until it appeared as if it unzipped the fabric of space and stepped into this area. This area was pitch black. Soulless, nerveless, skinless and organless had taken a toll on Ed. These processes have taken him beyond anything that any mortal could handle. They would have died at a thousand points at each stage. He still felt the pain from the four different extractions when a voice asked if he had any questions. Ed tried with all his might to get up but failed. He tried again but failed. Breathing heavy with his face on the smooth watery surface he tried again and made it to his knees. The voice asked again if Ed had any questions. The voice was old and croaky. It had a knowing edge to it. It had an heir of authority to it. It was a powerful voice. Ed couldn't speak after having his voice box ripped out with his oesophagus. The being had connected directly to Ed's mind and they communicated in a usual manner.

"Why are you doing this to me" said Ed in a cracking voice. The voice gave him that human connection that he had craved since he was shackled in the first realm.

"You deserve to be here" replied the voice.

"How? I am a family man?"

"What about your friends Ed?" "You sacrificed them to save yourself."

"They were criminals."

"And so were you."

"What has been happening to me?" said Ed.

The voice cackled. A light appeared and revealed a figure that was huge. It was nearly 20ft tall and slender it was covered in a black robe. The head was completely covered, and the robe was so long that it grouped around the floor. Long skeleton looking hands hung out of the bottom of the sleeves and one hand was holding a huge book. It was worn and looked leathery. It was a patch work of tan and various hues of brown but filthy.

"Ed, you are on a course to hell." It said.

Ed put his head in his hands and dry sobbed. It hit him like a ton of bricks.

"You entered the first chamber and came across Chesteez, the soul taker. You entered the second chamber and happened across Mulafsee the remover of nerves. The third chamber is Chinbukin's where your skin was cut off and your organs removed, and you met your bad deeds. Your bad deeds brought you here the fourth and final chamber. This is my domain, and I will enlighten you. I am Lerex and together we are the Caterers. We are the bridge to hell, we are the truth to bring you to justice for your deeds and we are vital in the equilibrium of existence."

"What is going to happen to me here?" said Ed with a solemn resignation. Here you will be relieved of your muscle, arteries and veins before you go forth into hell."

"I have been a good person and done nothing but loved and cared for my family. I have even been kind of religious." Ed said in the strongest voice he could muster. Boom! The floor shook as Lerex threw the book in front of Ed. It was as big and thick as a suitcase. Seeing it this close Ed could see that it was made out of skin. "How could you do this to people?" Ed's voiced cracked again as he began to dry sob again.

"There are many mysteries in the world that cannot be comprehended. This is due to mixed information attributed to different areas of the world, different time periods, different religions, different races, different modes of communication and many, many voices having a platform to get across their own message. Contradiction, science, education and a slipping belief in beyond the sight of eye. Your physicists have told you that dark matter is the majority of existence that the human realm consists of and still the human mind does not understand what has been explained for millennia. You have been shown some of what is and if you had behaved in accordance to the decree you would not be here. We are the Caterers to your degradation. We are the door you do not want to open. We know if you make amends. We know when and what actions condemn you as the Book screams when you are dead."
"You took solace in the comforting aspects of death over what seemed gruesome. You thought you may be taken on a gentle boat ride over still waters or come back as a butterfly maybe? No! You are here forever; this is your eternity and be forewarned that the practices that have been inflicted upon you are nothing of what is to come."
Ed's eyes grew wide with fear. He could not believe what Lerex had just said. How could things possibly get worse? This was confusing and filled him with dread. Just as this thought came to mind, Lerex quickly moved to the rear of Ed. He grabbed him by the top of his head with his

large bony hand and sliced him from the corner of his mouth to the back of his head with his sharp index finger. The zygomaticus major, buccinator, risorius and masseter were severed. Lerex dropped him, grabbed his upper and lower lip and peeled the muscle from his skull. The upper lip and surrounded muscles were ripped back right over the top of his head and both pulled down to his neck and left hanging like a hood. He pulled the triceps clean of the bone, then the pectoralis and latissimus dorsi. He ripped off the rest of the muscles like a mad gardener weeding his garden. Ed kicked and screamed as would a tot throwing a tantrum but Lerex was way too strong. Lerex discarded Ed out of his path like a rag doll. As he landed hard on the ground a short way away, the ground began to move. Ed tried to scramble to his feet but there were thousands of tiny spiders crawling all over him. He tried to squash and brush them off but there were too many. They were feasting on the tiny muscle, skin and blood fragments on his bones. They devoured his brain by making their way in through his nasal cavity, eye sockets and climbing his spinal column. He was throwing himself around, rolling around on the floor. He was clawing at his face as they were eating his eyeballs. At the sound of a horn blown at an earth shattering decibel, all the spiders disintegrated. Even though he was without any skin, organs, muscles, nerves or anything he could feel a different type of extreme heat. Even though his eyes had been taken he had a new form of sight.

Ed saw the floor was open and he could hear the shrillest of screams coming from the hole.
Even with no soul he could feel a different type of fear. With no brain he was thinking the worst.
Just stood there with his back to Ed. He didn't even look fully over his shoulder at him as he said "Take him."
A sound of feet pounding the ground began to crescendo. Snarling could be heard coming from the hole. Ed couldn't do anything when these shadows of some four-legged beasts emerged and dragged him into the fiery pit where he was going to face an eternity of suffering that would dwarf what he had been through. The last thing he heard from the fourth chamber was "You were forewarned not to sin. You were forewarned not to go against the decree. You. Were. Forewarned" followed by the cackle of Lerex.

THE END

Printed in Great Britain
by Amazon

44709657R00066